SPECIAL MESSAGE TO READERS

THE ULVERSCROFT FOUNDATION
(registered UK charity number 264873)

was established in 1972 to provide funds for research, diagnosis and treatment of eye diseases. Examples of major projects funded by the Ulverscroft Foundation are:-

- The Children's Eye Unit at Moorfields Eye Hospital, London
- The Ulverscroft Children's Eye Unit at Great Ormond Street Hospital for Sick Children
- Funding research into eye diseases and treatment at the Department of Ophthalmology, University of Leicester
- The Ulverscroft Vision Research Group, Institute of Child Health
- Twin operating theatres at the Western Ophthalmic Hospital, London
- The Chair of Ophthalmology at the Royal Australian College of Ophthalmologists

You can help further the work of the Foundation by making a donation or leaving a legacy. Every contribution is gratefully received. If you would like to help support the Foundation or require further information, please contact:

THE ULVERSCROFT FOUNDATION
The Green, Bradgate Road, Anstey
Leicester LE7 7FU, England
Tel: (0116) 236 4325

website: www.foundation.ulverscroft.com

JOHNNY DOLLAR

An orphaned child raised by a preacher and destined to run foul of the law, it's murder that keeps Johnny running, with trouble on his tail. In Julesville he finds a pretty schoolteacher set to win his love — but in the shadows, the Hellblazing Gang is waiting, determined to steal something more valuable than a man's heart. The gang holds a secret which is part of Johnny's past and the key to his future, and to gain his freedom Johnny Dollar has to pay a murderous price . . .

Books by Tony Masero
in the Linford Western Library:

JAKE RAINS

TONY MASERO

JOHNNY DOLLAR

Complete and Unabridged

LINFORD
Leicester

First published in Great Britain in 2012 by
Robert Hale Limited
London

First Linford Edition
published 2014
by arrangement with
Robert Hale Limited
London

*A catalogue record for this book is available
from the British Library.*

ISBN 978–1–4448–2031–7

Published by
F. A. Thorpe (Publishing)
Anstey, Leicestershire

Set by Words & Graphics Ltd.
Anstey, Leicestershire
Printed and bound in Great Britain by
T. J. International Ltd., Padstow, Cornwall

This book is printed on acid-free paper

For my son Ricci and his bride Rusty
May their time together be blessed
and their days happy ones

Prologue

The story they tell goes like this . . .

The outlaw Johnny Dollar was a reprehensible villain, an ex-convict, one time lawman, thief and killer who mercilessly shot down a man up in Polk County, Wisconsin and was subsequently hounded and gunned down himself by a sheriff's posse. It is also told that Johnny Dollar had two brothers and they all ran together with the Hellblazing Gang, causing great distress and privation to private persons and businesses in and around the country. But, like so many legends and myths of the Old West that have circulated since those days, there's barely an ounce of truth in it.

It never happened that way. If you really want to understand the nature of the man called Johnny Dollar and his true story you need a few cents' worth more than that. You have to go back to his origins.

Or maybe even just a little before . . . .

1

The National Steam Navigation Company's ironclad steamship SS *Princess*, weighed 3,000 tons, carried three masts and one funnel and managed ten knots from her single screw propulsion. Her manifest said 1,200 passengers but this was a woefully inaccurate total, as many more German emigrants had arrived from Antwerp just before sailing and they were to pick up even more at Queenstown in Ireland before heading on to New York.

It cost Pa Cable his small flock of sheep coming into their winter coat to pay for the crossing. When he and his young wife eventually boarded the emigrant vessel on the busy Liverpool docks, neither had ever seen the sea before, let alone travelled by boat. It was a fearsome event for them both as the ship hauled anchor and set sail, leaving their home and the English coastline behind for ever. Pa Cable, though, showed none of it, his grey eyes were as steely and hard as his nature and they hid his nervousness well. But his wife could not keep the troubled look from her gaze, nor the stiffness from her body. To calm her as the great ship rocked in the heaving swell once they had left the smoother waters of the Mersey, Pa in consideration took her across to an elderly seaman who stood leaning at the ship's side reaming out the bowl of his clay pipe with a small penknife and idly casting the dross to the wind.

'Excuse me, sir,' Pa Cable said. 'My wife here is troubled. She fears the rocking will tip us over and the seas shall overcome us. Or that some leviathan or sea monster shall rise up from the deep and swallow us as happened to poor Jonah in the Bible.'

The hoary old sailor looked them over and saw the distress in the wide innocent eyes of the young woman, who was a comely girl of healthy appearance and a pleasure to look upon with her cheeks reddened and dark hair tangled by the wind, and he took pity on her. He looked again into his pipe bowl and, satisfied, put it between his lips and blew down the stem to clear it. Taking his time the old man stuffed a wad of tobacco into the pipe and clenched it, bowl downwards, between his teeth before answering.

'Why no, young ma'am. See here, I have made this crossing five times, there and back and I still live. This old barque,' he slapped the wooden gunwale hard with a calloused palm for effect, 'is a trusty vessel. You have a good crew here and a strong captain, hard but fair. He'll see you through; don't upset yourself. We may get some weather but 'tis nothing to worry about. You'll reach the Americas safe and sound within a month or so. The cap'n will see to that.'

After three days at sea they learnt the

full measure of the captain's character for themselves.

The passengers were a mixed collection of nationalities from all across Europe, many with young families all intent on making a new start on the distant continent. One of the cabin passengers, a rakish Frenchman, was discovered attempting to force himself upon a young girl in one of the dark and gloomy steerage passageways. It was unsure whether the girl, who was no more than fourteen or fifteen, had led the man on precociously or if he had pressed himself upon her of his own volition. Be that as it might, the father of the girl, a stout and verbose man of Belgian origin and a religious inclination, was enraged and called loudly for the captain to mete out some form of justice for the alleged assault.

In answer, the captain, a grim, firm-jawed block of a man with a permanently downturned curve to his lips, called all the passengers to stand before him on the main deck. This included the few cabin passengers and most of the many in steerage, who crowded one on top of the other to get a better view. Then the captain set about questioning the Frenchman, who was held firmly upright before him between two of the crew.

'Well,' he growled. 'What have you to say for yourself?'

The Frenchman, something of an arrogant dandy, in ruffled shirt and cuffs under a long silk jacket, stood erect and apparently surprised by all the fuss. The man babbled away in French, having no English to speak of. Patiently the captain waited until the Frenchman had finished his long monologue and given a little enigmatic shrug of his shoulders in nonchalant conclusion. Then abruptly the captain took the Frenchman in his brawny bunched fist and dragged the struggling prisoner by his ruffles to the ship's side. Without further ado he threw him overboard.

Turning on his heel the captain

nodded at his first mate, then strode back to his cabin without a second glance at the shocked passengers. With a toothless grin the mate called out with finality 'There you have it,' and dispersed the gathering.

In such a way, the Cables discovered that, next to God, there was only the captain's word as law on the open sea. It was to be a callous introduction to the indifference they were to meet all too soon in their new home across the ocean, where an arbitrary form of justice was often dispensed from the barrel of a loaded six-gun or at a rope's end.

Although Pa Cable did note later in life that, as a result of the captain's act of peremptory justice, there was not a single further instance of trouble or complaint made during their time upon the water.

2

The Cables, who were virtually penniless, having spent all they had on the journey over, once processed through the immigration centre at Castle Garden found promised work amongst an English community occupying a small hamlet just outside New York. Pa worked as shepherd, which was his particular skill, and Ma as milkmaid. When the two had managed to save enough they took their leave of the farm and continued on their way inland in hope of a more promising way of life. Pa had constructed a flatbed wagon of sorts from a pair of old iron-hooped wheels and gash timber from a generous lumber yard. A long tongue with a wide crosspiece formed the handle and, after packing their few possessions, they set off pulling the wagon, one on each side of the crosspiece, making for the wagon train rendezvous where hopefuls were gathering for the trip overland.

They owned, in all, a canvas tent, some cooking utensils, an elderly Henry rifle with a pouch of .44 ammunition and a spare poke bonnet for Ma Cable to wear at church meetings. Other than that they had little more than the clothes they stood up in, and in such a way they set out on foot along with hundreds of others to make the overland journey to the promise of the lush Californian lands in the far West.

The year was 1866 and Ma was seventeen years old, her husband three years her senior.

Ma Cable was also pregnant by then, carrying their first child. Still, she took her turn at the wagon handle and steadily the two pulled their way across the intervening months as one of a train of Conestoga's bound into the wild country beyond civilization. During the approaching fall months they reached Wisconsin Territory and with the grey peaks of the Rockies in sight the young woman was delivered, with difficulty, of a young boy. They named him Adam, he being the first.

But Ma Cable suffered as a result of the birth and could not go on, her blood loss had been great and it was considered that for fear of death she should rest until able to continue. The wagon captain determined that unfortunately the train could not wait for them; winter was approaching and there were passes ahead that they must cross before the snow came and made them impassable.

A collection was made from amongst their fellow travellers and gifts of preserved foodstuffs, a long-handled axe, and hammer and nails and a skinning knife were made to the Cables. So it came about that the Cables were forced to settle short of their goal and set up camp near to a small outpost community called Duzacres. They found themselves a pleasant enough site beside a slow-flowing stream, one of those many that had given the place its original name when it had been settled by Spanish and Portuguese settlers many years before. The name had been corrupted from *Doze Aguas* for the twelve tributaries that ran in to the main river, which flowed near the small township.

The first winter they passed there was hard, with little protection from the chill snowy wind that blew down from the mountains. The two of them and the baby made the best of it in their canvas tent. Pa felled local pine with the axe and began to build a cabin as best he could. Eventually kindly neighbours came up from the township to their aid and by the spring the Cables had a birch-bark roof over their heads and some sort of cover from the wet weather that came with the new year.

One year later, Johnny was born, the second of the three sons that Ma was to bear. The youngest, fair-haired William soon called Billy Boy, arrived three years after Johnny.

The Cables worked hard at farming their land, growing beans, squash and sweet potato. Pa shot deer and rabbit with the Henry rifle and they traded what surplus they had until he could build up a small flock of sheep. From that came meat and also wool, which Ma carded and spun, selling the balls of wool to a Scots lady living in the town who knitted them into warm jumpers much treasured by the local population come the winter time.

Johnny Cable, a sturdy, open-faced boy was in a favoured position as the second child. Adam, the first, was much fussed over, as was the youngest sibling Billy Boy. But Johnny, the cleverest and most adventurous of the three, was left much to his own devices; when free he ran in the woods or swam and fished in the broad river's tributaries. They were all, in a way, allowed their freedom, as both parents worked hard over long hours with little time left for family. Even so, the boys learned from an early age to pull their weight and each had his daily task to fulfil, whether it was fetching water from the stream, guarding the sheep or weeding out the cabin's vegetable garden. There was no schooling and as the older Cables could not read or write the education the boys received was one of a more practical nature.

At last Pa Cable was able to afford a plough and a workhorse and it was with proud joy that he set about clearing and preparing a field for planting on a larger scale. He had corn in mind, and a small patch set aside for tobacco. Johnny was eleven years old at this time, Adam twelve and Billy Boy nine. They were all healthy, lively boys. Adam tended to plumpness and laziness, but the youngest, Billy Boy, was a soft, quiet child, and they all had to admit he was a mite simple into the bargain. Johnny was without doubt the brightest, most alert and of an independent nature. In appearance he was marked with his mother's unruly dark hair and good looks.

* * *

It was Johnny, bringing the lunch pail, who found him.

Pa Cable lay in the third furrow that he had managed to carve out with his new plough. No one could tell whether he had stumbled and fallen over the newly turned earth and stunned himself on a rock, and that the long guide traces he kept looped over both shoulders had tangled and stretched his neck as surely as a hangman's noose when the horse had continued stolidly plodding along. Either that or his heart had just given out after all the years of continuous labour. Whatever the cause, Pa Cable was dead and the family left without a bread-winner.

Ma Cable struggled on. The boys were forced to try to follow in their father's footsteps as they managed the flock, hunted, and maintained the large vegetable patch. But it was an uphill struggle and soon the plough and the horse were sold off and the cleared field forgotten. Then the sheep went down with white muscle disease and three winters later Ma Cable caught a severe chill whilst breaking ice to fetch water in a freezing gale. Pale and weakened, she died within a month, coughing up thin streaks of blood from her damaged lungs.

Johnny walked the miles into Duzacres alone and took the news to the town council, a group of five elders. Their nominal leader, Blue Pennyfeather, was a forty-one-year-old man who was recognized as town mayor more by general consensus than by any legal vote. He was a likeable, quiet and self-effacing fellow, who avoided confrontation and often deferred to the more vigorously expressed ideas of a fearsome, heavily bearded man called Jacob Inx. Inx had newly arrived in town from the East, forcefully claiming that he was a properly ordained minister of the church and was sent to bring the Word of God to the frontier. With a missionary zeal he took to leading the weekly services and although not a popular figure the congregation was pleased to have at last a man of God in their small community. A town meeting was called at his behest and all the townsfolk and outlying farmers attended to decide what to do about the three boys who were now bereft of parental care and attention.

Preacher Inx held the meeting in his parlour, where the people filled the room and spilled out into the street outside. Spring was approaching and the worst of winter over, so for those outside it was not too unpleasant. A jug was passed round to mitigate any chill and as a result the meeting in the road outside soon developed a more cheery air than that inside.

The preacher, dressed in black broadcloth and wearing his broad-brimmed hat, as he did at all times, took control of things with barely a nod of recognition of Blue Pennyfeather's position. He was an overbearing man who confidently believed he led the congregation by divine right and was guided in all things by a higher authority, which spoke directly to the churchgoers through his mouth.

'Neighbours!' he called, begging for silent attention. 'You all know the purpose. These here poor orphans are without home or hearth.' He waved an encompassing hand over the three boys, who stood in embarrassed silence before the collective gaze of their neighbours. They felt like lost sheep about to be sold on the auctioneer's block. 'Their folks were hardworking and honest, so there's no bad blood to be found here. I see fine young men in the making and it is God's will that we should offer them succour. Now, are there any here who will take these boys into their care?'

Widow Jenkins, a plump and ugly woman, with unsightly moles and whiskers on her face raised a tentative hand. 'I'm willing to take one o' them. My poor hubby passed without leaving me no chillen to love and attend, and I'll be glad to fill that gap with one o' these poor mites. For I have long wished to play at mother and it'd be a blessing to have one to care for me in my old age, right enough.'

Preacher Inx nodded benignly. 'Bless you, Sister Jenkins. God's love fills you now. Which of these lost ones will you take to your own?'

'Why that one there,' she said, pointing at the tall, tubby figure of Adam, who, at twelve years of age looked to be more a young man than a boy. 'He seems a fine, well-built specimen.'

Adam was duly ushered forward and with a dazed look was enfolded into the ample bombazine bosom of the smiling Widow Jenkins, who, one might have thought, was perhaps guided by an intention other than plain charity as her lidded eyes flicked in secret appraisal over young Adam's sturdy physique. A round of soft applause followed her show of charity and the Widow Jenkins rose an inch or two in stature at the recognition.

'Now then,' said the preacher. 'Anybody else?'

'Dis vun, I vill haff dis vun. He haf de blond hair and vill match mine udder children.' It was the strapping *hausfrau*, Helda Gunther who spoke out, ignoring her husband standing beside her, a small and, as everybody knew, henpecked wisp of a man. She had already brought ten children into the world and all wondered how such a frail husband kept pace with the demands of this monumental woman. Her finger pointed unerringly in Billy Boy's direction.

The nine-year-old Billy Boy looked doubtful and his lip began to tremble as the implications sunk in. Preacher Inx put a fatherly hand on his shoulder. 'Don't weep now, boy. This good woman has offered you a home where you have none. Be grateful and praise the Lord in thanksgiving.'

Johnny Cable looked over at his

younger brother and felt a pang of sympathy run through him at the sight of his tearstained cheeks. 'We have to be split up, Preacher?' he asked. 'My brothers and me, we'd kinda like to stay together.'

'Not possible, boy,' intoned the preacher. 'More mouths to feed and no one here has the wherewithal to fit three growing boys at their table. You'll see your kin from time to time, I'm sure.' With that he roughly pushed little Billy Boy in the direction of Mrs Gunther, who grasped the child's wrist in her hand and pulled him into her voluminous skirts. Billy Boy let out a terrified wail of fear as the dark cloth enclosed him. 'Dere,' said Mrs Gunther. 'Be a gutt boy and dere vill be apfel pie for you at home.' The promise of such bounty did something to moderate Billy Boy's tears; he had not eaten much for the past few days, and his wailing was reduced to a low snivelling.

'Now there is one left,' called the

preacher. 'Who amongst you will offer this lad a home?'

Johnny frowned at the silence that followed, it was as if a knowledge of the boy's independence passed unspoken around the room. Those present had experienced Johnny's wit and intelligence and recognized a handful when they saw one. No one was prepared to take on the challenge.

'No one?' asked the preacher after a few minutes had passed. 'Come, surely one amongst you has a heart big enough?'

Silence and a nervous rustle of embarrassment followed his words. Those at the back were already quietly slipping out through the door and taking their leave.

'Well,' sighed Preacher Inx, 'if none will, then it behoves myself and my lady wife to take on the burden. Alice?' he turned questioningly to his wife, a small, thin, pinch-faced, childless woman, dressed similarly all in black. She jerked her head once, as a bird might and fixed a bright, beady eye, on Johnny.

'Come here, boy,' she ordered, in a tone sharp as a knife blade scraping on china plate. She reached out her bony hand.

Johnny stood rooted to the spot, not wishing one iota to be taken into the preacher's fold. As the congregation had silently recognized his own innate challenging nature, so he too instinctively understood the imprisoning world that was beckoning in that outstretched hand. Preacher Inx covered Johnny's hesitation by clamping a large hand around the back of the boy's neck and pushing him forcefully in his wife's direction.

'There, lad. We take you into the bosom of our family.' Once Johnny was safely deposited at his wife's side the preacher turned again to the gathered crowd. 'It is done, brethren. God's work is done this night. May you all depart in blessed peace and we shall gather again on Sunday next to praise the Lord and His many works. Blessings be upon you and good night to all.'

3

It did not take Johnny long to find out how things would be from now on. It started next morning with a meagre crust of dry bread and a battered tin mug of milk. Then came a list of tasks that were daunting for the youngster. Mrs Inx proved to be a veritable taskmaster and followed her husband's lead in assuring Johnny that everything was for the good of his own soul. What Johnny could not understand, though, was how slopping out the hog pen brought him any closer to his Maker.

* * *

An exhausting three years passed.

By that time the fourteen-year-old had had enough. One evening he stood grim-faced and determined before the preacher and his wife in their dining room. He was now on the edge of adulthood and a certain awareness of his own self-worth was beginning to fill his consciousness. As a farm boy he knew the labour expected of him and was not afraid of such hard work, but the never-ending menial and petty tasks laid upon him by the preacher's wife verged suspiciously on the edge of slavery and this offended his dignity.

For this reason, although his clothes were now stained and torn and mud streaked his face, he stood before them proudly.

'You want something Johnny?' asked Preacher Inx, looking up from his supper plate.

'You intend I should work like this each and every day, year in and out for the rest of my days?' asked the boy.

'Why, 'tis no more than a way to earn your keep, Johnny. A healthy outdoor life and strong work hurt no man.'

'If it's earning my keep I am, then I reckon I should be paid for it, wouldn't you say?' Johnny asked him belligerently.

The preacher laughed, a nasty, unkind bark, and cast a sidelong glance at his wife, who stared with icy keenness at Johnny. 'And just what do you think you should earn above your food and lodging, pray tell?'

'I reckon a dollar a week is fair pay for what you're asking of me.'

'A dollar a week! You hear that, Alice? A dollar a week, why bless me! You have a nerve indeed, young Johnny. To stand before those who have taken you under their wing, given you a roof when you had none, and now you expect payment for the few tasks that are asked of you.'

'A dollar a week,' Johnny insisted.

Alice Inx fixed Johnny with eyes that glittered like two black gemstones. 'This boy needs chastising, husband,' she hissed malevolently.

'Indeed,' said the preacher, rising from his chair. 'I believe you are right, wife.'

'T'ain't much,' said Johnny firmly, standing his ground. 'A dollar is all I'm asking.'

'Well, I'll give you a dollar's worth all

right,' snapped the preacher, lunging forward and grasping Johnny by the arm. 'You come along o' me to the woodshed, Johnny Dollar. Let's see how a paddling with my leather belt suits you.'

Alice Inx allowed a tight smile to slide across her mean face. 'Johnny Dollar,' she said. 'Never a truer name put to it. Wilful and precocious child, thinking only of your own selfish gain instead of the gracious Christian charity you receive. 'Johnny Dollar', it well suits one whose greedy thoughts are motivated only by the prospect of cash money.'

The woodshed at the rear of the building was more of a barn than a shed. As Preacher Inx pushed Johnny through the double doors, the boy smelt the fresh pine logs he had cut and stacked earlier that week, mixed with the scent of the horse the preacher kept there. The pony whickered nervously as they entered, sensing that all was not well.

'Now,' said Preacher Inx, unstrapping the belt from his waist. 'I expect you to take this like a man, Johnny.' It was an old, broad, leather belt, thick and worn to a soft flexibility. 'Go take hold of that stall post there,' the preacher ordered. 'I'm about to give you a whipping you won't forget, boy. But you will remember to treat me with respect from now on, especially in front of my lady wife. To whom you will apologize once I have finished with you.'

He swung back his arm and swooped the leather across Johnny's back with a stinging thwack. 'Remember, boy. How the Lord Jesus took his whipping. Without complaint and with only loving kindness for those who struck him.'

Wincing in pain, Johnny leant down and picked up the wooden feed bucket at his feet. It was a heavy object and when he swung it up and it connected hard with the preacher's chin it made a satisfying hollow clunk. The preacher stumbled backwards, stunned and surprised. Johnny followed after him.

'Beat me like a dog, would you?' hissed Johnny, bringing the bucket down hard again. The preacher's head swung away sideways at the blow and his knees began to buckle and give under him. Johnny hit him again and again, a righteous rage fuelling his attack. 'You sanctimonious old duffer, you'll never strike me again!' he shouted as he continued to rain swinging blows down on the preacher's head.

Bloody and unconscious, the preacher slid down to the straw-strewn earthen floor. Johnny stood panting over him. His eye roamed down to the waistcoat and the gold watch chain looped there. Leaning down with a snarl Johnny snatched it from the waistcoat pocket. It was a heavy gold hunter with an ornate flip lid covering the face.

'There, Preacher. A tad more than a dollar's worth but I reckon I've got it coming.' He pushed the watch and chain into his trouser pocket and turned to look at the stabled pony.

'That horse too, I think, Mr Inx. I'll need a stretch of distance between you and me before this night's out. That witch in there will pay merry hell with my reputation before she's done, I'm damned sure of that.' Johnny gave the preacher a last kick in the ribs, caught up the hanging saddle and blanket and made his way over to the fretting pony.

4

Johnny was sitting on the edge of the boardwalk when they took him. A tall, pale-faced, shabbily dressed man, he was quite ordinary looking really, but he wore a crudely cut metal star in the middle of his pushed-out crown hat and an oiled leather gunbelt with a bone-handled pistol high on his waist. The gunbelt looked like the only thing he cared for and that was the one thing that signalled cause for concern to Johnny.

Johnny had travelled the best part of 160 miles of rough country over the past two days. When he arrived on the night of the second day in Crosstrees, a busy township set at the foot of the mountains both he and the horse were exhausted. Johnny had managed to sell the gold watch and chain to a fellow in a saloon and had bought a meal for himself and feed for the pony. Then, after tying the pony to a hitching rail, Johnny had fallen asleep, leaning against a post set in the boardwalk. It was the peace officer's boot in his thigh that had awoken him.

'This here yours?' the sheriff asked, raising questioning eyes in the direction of the dust-caked pony tied to the rail. Johnny cleared his eyes with the knuckles of both hands.

'Sure is,' he croaked, his mouth and throat dry from sleep.

The sheriff looked across doubtfully at his deputy, an ill-clad, unshaven fellow who cradled a Winchester long rifle in the crook of his arm. The sheriff turned back to Johnny. 'What's that brand on the rump then?' he asked.

Johnny paused. He had no idea.

'Is there an 'I' in it somewhere?' he ventured. 'I just bought the critter from a fellow so I ain't so sure.'

'That a fact,' said the sheriff with a smirk.

Johnny had been making for a cut in

the high mountains. A deep-sided valley provided the main route through the range and the passing trade meant that the township was a large and busy place. Johnny had hoped his passing through would go unnoticed in the press of activity.

'What's your name, young fella?' the sheriff asked.

'Er . . . Johnny Dollar.'

'Well, you come along o' us, Johnny Dollar. Unless you got a bill of sale, 'cause there ain't no brand set on that pony and I think you done stole the beast.'

Slowly Johnny got to his feet, thinking fast. 'I ain't got no bill of sale 'cause the fellow who sold it couldn't write none.'

'Sure thing, boy,' said the sheriff cynically. 'You know what? I think you're a runaway and you lit out with this here pony and your pa's gold watch. Oh, yeah . . . ' he said looking into Johnny's round eyes. 'We heard about that and read what was wrote inside the lid too. *Preacher Jacob Inx, from a grateful congregation,* that's what it said. Now, you don't look one bit like no preacher man so where you from, son? You tell us so we can advise your folks you're all right.'

Johnny hung his head and would not answer.

'That's the way of it, huh?' the sheriff said, in a not unkindly fashion. 'Your pa one o' those fire-and-brimstone old boys who comes down hard on their children?'

'My pa's dead,' Johnny answered sullenly.

'Well,' the sheriff shrugged, 'if you stole this pony from a preaching man, my guess is it'll go hard with you once he finds out you're here. Now get along there. Walk in front of us down to the jailhouse, we'll see the horse gets stabled 'til its owner collects.'

A small crowd of curious early risers was beginning to gather as Johnny walked ahead of the lawmen down the centre of the street.

'What you got there, Sheriff Mayhew?' one called out.

'You go about your business,' the sheriff answered coolly. 'Nothing to pay no heed to. Just a runaway boy is all.'

'Where's he from?' another asked.

'Won't say,' answered the sheriff. 'Any of you people travelling east of here, spread the word. I'm looking for a preacher. Name of Jacob Inx. Tell him we got this boy and his horse here. His gold watch he'll have to go whistle for, though. Man paid good money for that and he ain't parting with it.'

They entered the wood-plank jailhouse. The first thing Johnny noticed in the gloomy interior was the unpleasant scent of unwashed feet and stale urine. An unoccupied iron barred cage was set to one side of the small room. A littered desk stood at the opposite end with a cold pot-bellied stove next to it in the corner. Two wooden benches stood against the free corner where little heaps of unswept dust gathered around a battered brass spittoon.

'Ain't much but it's home,' quipped the sheriff as they entered. 'You get the cage, Johnny Dollar. You got a blanket in there, none too clean I know, but that's all we got. Do your necessaries in the bucket there, which you empties out personal each morning. We got a pump out back where you can wash up too if you feel so inclined. Sad to say, most of our customers tend to ignore that particular facility. Now, I ain't going to put no manacles on you if you behave. You fuss or try anything and I'll chain you up, y'hear?'

Sadly, Johnny entered the cage. He heard the door clang to behind him and a key turn in the lock.

The sheriff tested the locked door and said. 'I'm Sheriff Ira Mayhew and this here is my deputy Chad Wilder. Just so you know who to call.'

'Sheriff?' said Johnny.

'Uhuh?'

'I really got to stay in here?'

'Sure do, boy. You stole a horse and that's a capital crime in these parts, same as most elsewhere. Sorry to see a youngster like you in such a situation but that's the law and I wouldn't be doing my duty I didn't lock you up.'

'Seems a mite mean, is all,' Johnny said, putting on his most mournful look. 'I only got fourteen years.'

'Wrong is wrong, Johnny. You know that. Now you done the crime and you got to pay for it, so just get on with it and don't give me none of that weepy-eyed stuff. Y'hear?'

Johnny went over to the iron bunk and sat down heavily, stunning his rump when he found there was no mattress, only flat metal bars running across under the blanket.

'Don't you take it so hard,' piped up the deputy, in a high-pitched Southern accent. 'Maybe you'll just get some prison time is all. Be out and about in a few years. Think on it.'

Johnny knew they were just trying to be kind and set him at rest, but their forecast did little to ease his troubled mind and he dropped his despairing head in his hands.

5

When Preacher Inx eventually arrived he still wore the effects of his beating beneath a bundle of swathed bandages that covered a yellowish bruised eye and swollen jaw. He was not a happy man.

'You have the dad-blasted felon here?' he bawled as he entered, bursting into the jailhouse without overture.

Sheriff Mayhew rose slowly from behind his desk and asked calmly. 'You are . . . ?'

'I'm the preacher for Duzacres. Jacob Inx. I received word you hold the recalcitrant young beggar in your custody. Set about me and stole from me, the ungrateful wretch.'

'That him there?' asked Mayhew, indicating Johnny, who was sitting despondent in the corner cage.

'That's the one,' bellowed Inx.

'Well, sir,' said the sheriff. 'We hold your horse in the livery stable. He's yours to claim once you've paid the stabling fee. As to the prisoner, you can either charge him here for adjudgement or take him back with you and see to it in your own county. That's your choice.'

'Oh!' growled Inx angrily. 'I'll take him back with me, have no fear on that.'

'Well, sir. I have to tell you that in that case he'll be in your care. I can't afford to part with my deputy for the transport.'

'But Sheriff. The boy's a danger to all. Look what he did to me. Cracked my skull open in his wildness. The cursed boy's a murderer in the making.'

'So I see, Preacher. Still, I can't let my man go with you, I need him here.'

'Hot damn, Sheriff. That's a grave inconvenience.'

Sheriff Mayhew drew himself up and frowned. 'Begging your pardon, sir, but you sure use a lot of strong words for a preacher man. I'd be obliged if you'd tone down your language a mite.'

Preacher Inx huffed and swallowed his anger with difficulty. 'I do apologize, Sheriff. I fear I am forgetting myself. This unfortunate incident has upset me enormously. Pray forgive me.'

Mayhew nodded silently and picked up the cage keys.

'My watch?' Inx asked suddenly. 'My gold watch, he stole it. It was a treasured item, a gift from my last parish.'

'The boy sold it. You might still find the buyer over at the saloon if he hasn't lit out. Cost you, though. The man wasn't keen to part with her.'

Preacher Inx bit back another curse and fumed, his eyes darting at Johnny with vengeful meanness.

'You want to take the boy now?' asked Mayhew.

'Can you at least shackle him?'

' 'Fraid not. We have but the one pair of irons and frequent calls on them here.'

'Dammit, Sheriff!' Inx hissed, again

forgetting himself for the moment.

Mayhew looked across at him with an icy glance. 'I told you once to mind your manners. Now watch your words, mister, or I'll pistol-whip you myself. I'm beginning to see now why this lad took off.'

Inx shrunk inside himself, the lowering of his eyes speaking volumes, although he said nothing as Mayhew crossed to the cage and unlocked the door.

'Come on, Johnny Dollar,' said the sheriff. 'Time to go.'

As Johnny made his slow way out of the pen, Inx leapt forward and grasped him by the scruff of the neck.

'Johnny Dollar, indeed,' he hissed. 'If they won't give me irons, then I'll hogtie you and you'll walk the 160 miles back to Duzacres.'

Sheriff Mayhew looked at Johnny sadly. He was a hard man but not unreasonable. 'You take care now, Johnny Dollar. Don't let it get you down, y'hear?'

The preacher kept his promise once they reached the livery stables: he tied Johnny's hands before him and looped a noosed rope around his neck, which he ran through a stall-post ring. Then he emptied Johnny's pockets of the remaining money he had made from the sale of the watch and left him in the care of the stablehand whilst he went to see if he could reacquire his precious timepiece.

The hayseed who cared for the livery was a wan young fellow with unkempt hair who spoke little. He watched Johnny with dumb curiosity for a long while whilst leaning on his pitchfork handle.

'What you looking at?' Johnny eventually asked.

'I gotta watch you. I get a silver dollar fee if I keep you close by.'

Johnny recognized the tone of the childlike voice; it reminded him of his little brother Billy Boy. He fully realized the similarity and saw that the young man had as much wit as the post he was tied to. Then, as more of a joke than any serious attempt at escape, he said, 'You realize he'll give you two dollars to let me go though.'

The young man's face wrinkled into a studied frown as he worked on that one. 'You reckon?' he asked. 'How so?'

'Sure,' said Johnny, seeing a chink of light. 'Stands to reason, don't it? A silver dollar to keep me here and two of them to set me free.'

'I suppose,' said the stablehand, his brow lightening as the bizarre logic of it sunk in.

'Think on it,' urged Johnny. 'One to keep but two to let go.'

The boy nodded. 'Yeah, yeah. I see it. One to keep, two to let go.' He began to repeat the words as if they were a litany.

'Well?' asked Johnny, getting impatient. 'You going to do it?'

'All right, I think I will.' The stablehand dropped his pitchfork and fetched a long machete blade from a corner table. 'You've gotta promise me something, though,' he said as he laid the knife-edge across Johnny's bonds.

'What's that?'

'That you won't run off.'

'You've got it, partner,' Johnny promised with fervour.

* * *

The preacher's downfall was that he was newly arrived at the frontier and was too full of himself by far. His conviction that he was a heaven sent messenger of God denied him a clear understanding of those outside any Christian calling. So when he proudly entered the Bull Brand saloon and announced in a loud voice that if the owner of a certain stolen gold hunter would come forward he would reimburse him fully for the return to its lawful owner, his entreaty was met with a stony silence.

Preacher Inx looked around the room and saw before him a gathering of hardy bull-whippers who hauled freight through the pass, and various itinerant travellers and ladies of shady character, all enveloped in a cloud of tobacco smoke laced with the vinegary odour of spilled liquor.

'Come along now,' he called in his best pulpit voice. 'To steal is against the God Almighty's commandment. Let the man who is in possession come forward or himself be a part of the crime.'

A grizzled customer seated alone at a corner table growled back, 'Who you calling a thief, mister?' He was a heavy-set man, dressed in dirty fringed buckskins with a large horn-handled knife jutting from an Indian bead-patterned belt.

'You are the man?' asked Inx.

'Don't matter who I am,' answered the fellow. 'Who the hell are you to come busting in here accusing folk?'

Inx faltered a little at the aggressive tone of the man. 'I, sir, am Preacher Inx of Duzacres and am in search of a certain stolen gold watch of mine that the sheriff advises me was sold to a person in this establishment.'

'Inx? What in damnation is that the name of? Inx? It sounds like something you take a dip pen and write with more than a human body's name.'

There was a chorus of chuckles from around the room and Inx bridled at the pun. 'You, fellow, are before a man of God and I'll ask you to hold respect and take some care in your words.'

'Or you'll whop my sinful hide good, huh, Preacher? Bring down the wrath of the angelic army on me? Seems to me some little devil already come down hard on you as it is.' The trapper laughed.

Inx inadvertently touched his bandaged head. 'I . . . I was set on by the thief and it does not bode well for him, believe me.'

'Don't bode well for you either, you don't shut up and clear out of here. Ain't no place for your sort, 'specially ones with a loud voice and harsh words. So, go on, get along before I see you off myself.'

Inx drew a deeply determined breath. 'I'll leave when my business is attended to. Now, are you the man who has my pocket watch?'

The trapper rose slowly from his seat. As he moved he slid the long broad-bladed knife from its sheath. 'Get along, Preacher. I won't tell you again.'

As the man rose, Inx saw the glint of a gold chain looped over the bead belt. 'You have it!' he cried. 'There, I see it. You have my watch.'

' 'Tain't yours no more. I paid good for this.'

Inx bustled forward, his desire to acquire his possession driving sense from his head. 'Give it to me this instant . . . ' he cried. The words died in his throat as he felt the needle sharp prick of the knifepoint part his thick beard and press up under his chin.

'Or you'll do what?' asked the trapper, leaning pugnaciously forward and breathing whiskey-soaked fumes into the preacher's face.

Inx folded. He backed away nervously. 'I'll . . . I'll . . . ' he mumbled. 'I'll be getting along now.'

'Sure you will,' The trapper nodded, looking around confidently at the grinning faces in the room.

From the swing-gate door Inx turned. He could not miss out on making one parting gesture of defiance in return for the snub. His voice shook with the shame and indignation he felt as he cried out for all to hear.

'A curse on you, you rascal. As a minister of the Divine Word I bring down heaven's curse on you. May all the demons of Hell follow you from now on until the day you die.' Then, satisfied that he had had the last word, Inx turned on his heel and hurried off.

Whilst the occupants of the saloon laughed uproariously, the trapper, whose name was Edgar Freemantle, twisted his lips and frowned darkly. It was lucky for the preacher that he did not see the look that followed him.

For, although not a God-fearing man the trapper was of a deeply superstitious nature. Edgar Freemantle was not a fellow who took such a curse lightly. Not lightly at all.

6

'Nah,' said the stable hand, slowly raising the blade away from the rope. 'You're fooling with me.' He smiled broadly and gave Johnny a knowing look. 'You thought you could go sly on old Jeb, didn't you?'

'How so?' asked Johnny hurriedly, realizing that his opportunity was slipping away.

'I see it plain. You ain't going to stick around the minute I set you free, are you?'

'Hey, two dollars is two dollars, ain't it?'

Jeb shook his head. 'I don't think so. That man said one silver dollar. He said, one silver dollar to keep an eye on you. He never said nothing about two dollars and if I let you go free I can't keep my eye on you, can I?'

'Come on, bud,' begged Johnny. 'Just

you slice through them ropes and think no more about it.'

'Can't do that.' Jeb was suddenly obstinate, he turned away and returned the machete to its corner.

Preacher Inx burst into the stables and Johnny knew his chance at escape was lost.

'I watched him,' cried Jeb enthusiastically. 'I watched him like you said.'

'Fine,' answered Inx brusquely. Johnny could see he was flustered, his features were red and his actions hurried. 'Get my pair saddled up and hurry about it.'

'What about my dollar? You promised me a silver dollar,' insisted the stable-boy.

'Yes, yes,' hissed Inx, fumbling in his coat pocket. He took out a small, jingling, clasped purse, delved inside and tossed the boy a coin. 'Here, now get those saddles on. Johnny, you'll take the mount I came in on. I want no trouble with you, so just do as I say.'

Johnny wondered what had caused

the preacher's urgency and guessed that all had not gone according to plan in the saloon. He remembered the rough trapper fellow he had sold the watch to and pictured Inx's attitude, demanding and arrogant. He had to smile to himself as he realized the reason for Inx's desire for speed.

'Get your watch back, Preacher?' he asked innocently.

Inx glowered at him. 'Fellow wouldn't sell it,' he snapped. 'But you'll pay for that when I get you back to Duzacres.'

'Reckon I will,' Johnny answered grimly as Inx loosed his neck-noose from the post.

'I'm keeping you on this rope end and your hands tied, so you better keep up with me. You understand?'

Inx dug his heels into the lead mount and they set off with a softly called ''Bye,' from the stableboy. They rode fast out of town, away from the glowing sunset and into a darkening sky. Johnny clutched the saddle horn with his bound hands whilst Inx's urgent tugging dragged at the noose around his neck and forced him to keep pace with the preacher.

Fellow's scared, Johnny thought. *That old trapper must have blown a wind of fear on him*. He thumped his heels into the pony's ribs, drawing closer to the preacher and slackening the drag rope between them. *Lord!* Johnny continued to muse, *how in hell's name am I going to get out of this?*

The darkness thickened and as they left the well-used roadway close to town, the way ahead became more difficult to see in the dimming light. A treeline soon enclosed them, making the roadway even more obscure. There was no moon up this night and the way forward appeared as a pitch-black wall.

'Dammit!' Johnny heard the preacher curse. He ploughed on for another mile and when low-lying branches swept the hat from his head the preacher reined in. He dismounted and hunted around until he found the hat. When it was safely back on his head he pulled Johnny from the saddle.

'Get on down. We'll have to rest up until daylight. It's as black as the devil's armpit out here.'

Johnny liked the darkness; if the chance came his escape would be cloaked by the shadows. But the preacher looped the long rope around him and a tree trunk before he hobbled the ponies and sat down in fuming silence a little way off.

'Ain't you going to light a fire?' Johnny asked.

'No,' growled Inx. 'Too much danger of Indians about.'

'Hadn't heard of any war parties on the loose,' Johnny continued to prod. He knew full well that the preacher was more concerned about an irate trapper following them than any painted savages.

'Just be quiet,' snapped the preacher.

'Is there something else, Preacher? You seem awful worried.'

'Be still, Johnny. I have the Lord with me. I am safe from all harm; He is my shield and my saviour. The strong arm wherein I rest.'

The preacher mumbled on, praying to himself in order to keep his fears at bay.

'Was an awesome fellow, that trapper. Weren't he, Preacher?'

'What? What you say?' The preacher started.

'That trapper. Man with your pocket watch. Had that big old knife in his belt. You see that, Mr Inx?'

'Yes,' Inx answered vaguely.

'I think he was a mean man, that one,' Johnny went on, stirring the pot a little more. 'Would think nothing of creeping up on a person in his bed and slitting his throat.'

Johnny could almost hear the preacher turn to face him in the darkness. 'You think I fear such a man, Johnny Cable?' he almost shouted. 'I am strong in the Lord, I tell you. Who am I to be feared of such a sinner?'

Johnny knew his words were having their effect and that, for all his bluster the preacher was shivering in his boots at that moment.

'I'm sure you ain't a tad bit scared, Preacher. Just saying that such a man would think little of doing bad deeds at night. Trained hunter like that, probably sees like a cat in the dark.'

There was a rustle as the preacher adjusted himself. 'Best stop your prattling, Johnny, or I shall tie a cloth gag across your mouth.'

'Sorry, sir. Just I'm a bit afeared, I guess. Us alone out here in this wild country with no pistol or protection between us.'

'We have all the angels of heaven to watch over us.' Inx sighed doubtfully.

Johnny lapsed into silence and allowed the preacher to stew awhile. The silence grew longer and before Johnny even knew it he slept and then it was morning.

7

When Johnny awoke he saw the preacher laid out on his side with his back to him and apparently still fast asleep. With some difficulty he slid and wriggled ferociously, feeling the bonds that bound him to the tree riding up and down. There was some looseness there. Trying to be as quiet as possible he worked his slender body slowly down through the loops and eventually free of the rope. Although his wrists were still tied tightly in front of him he knew that if he could make it over to the ponies and unhobble one he would still be able to mount up and ride away. The Preacher continued to lie there undisturbed as Johnny crept over to the grazing animals. Bridles and saddles were lying nearby and, wincing at each tiny, sound Johnny managed to get one of the ponies fit to travel. It was hard with bound wrists: they were raw where the rope chafed. Then at last he was up and, from the height of the saddle and with a tight grin of satisfaction Johnny looked down on his tormentor for the last time.

That's when he saw the blood.

The grass was thick with it. It lay all around the preacher's head in a wide dark stain. Johnny hurriedly dismounted and went over to the supine figure. He was dead, that was for sure. His neck had been opened from ear to ear by a single long slash. Johnny had heard nothing whilst he slept but it seemed all his fancies of the night before had now become a reality. It was true that it could have been anybody in the night, either road agent or wild Indian, but Johnny guessed it had been the trapper with the bone-handled knife. The man had come upon them in the darkness bent on his silent mission of vengeance.

Johnny stood for a moment, biting his lip in troubled despair as he looked down at the body. It would go badly for him, he knew it. Everyone would think it had been he who'd committed the act. With some reluctance, he knelt and began to rifle the preacher's pockets. The purse with the silver dollars was gone but he did find a small pocket-knife and with this managed to saw through the rope at his wrists.

Johnny knew he had to hide the body and get as far away as possible as quickly as he could. It would not be long before the preacher's witch wife would raise the alarm and then people would be searching the road from Duzacres all the way back to Cross-trees. He dragged the corpse as deeply as possible amongst the surrounding trees and undergrowth, hoping that wild beasts would make fast work in disposing of it. He laid out the preacher in a fitting position with his arms folded across his chest and his broad-brimmed hat laid across his face. He had hated the man, that was true, but still he had not wished such an end to him. With a silent prayer for the repose of the preacher's soul Johnny quickly mounted and, bringing the spare horse behind, headed back the way he had come.

There was only one route he could follow now and that was up through the mountain pass and into the unknown lands beyond. Even now he might fulfil his parents' earlier dream, he realized, and make his way across to California, a place wide enough, he reckoned, to get lost in.

* * *

It was an Indian army scout who discovered the body. He had seen the birds of prey circling lazily over the treeline from a mile away and known they marked out a place of death. The relief cavalry troop he scouted for were on their way to the mountain pass at Crosstrees and then on to Fort Bendix, situated on the far side, where it was reported that restless bands of Bannock and Shoshoni were raiding.

The captain, Loren Edwards, an experienced veteran of the Civil War, in which he had fought with distinction, took immediate heed of the Indian's warning. He detailed two men to go off with the scout and discover the cause of the wheeling birds. So it was a mere two hours after Johnny's departure that the body was found.

The patrol carried the remains with them into Crosstrees and reported their find to Sheriff Ira Mayhew, who shook his head sadly as he recognized the preacher.

'You know the man?' asked Captain Edwards, as they studied the body laid out under a slicker on the boardwalk.

Mayhew nodded. 'Sure do. He was here just yesterday.'

'Looks like he might have been a man of the church,' observed the captain, taking out a cigar case and offering the sheriff one.

'Er, no thankee, Captain. Yep, he was a preacher. Must have been right good in the pulpit sure enough, for he certainly made a lot of noise.'

The captain snorted a laugh. 'You think that may have been what got him into this trouble?'

'He had a boy with him. A runaway, I reckon the preacher didn't treat him too well so that's probably how it panned out like this.'

'Too bad,' said the captain, setting fire to his stogie. 'You going to track him down, Sheriff?'

Mayhew nodded, 'That's my job.'

'Well, me and my men are headed through the pass. We'll keep an eye out. My Indian there is a hell of a scout. We'll send you a holler we spot the lad. What's he look like?'

'Dark-haired boy. Fourteen years, no hat, wearing a work shirt and dungarees that have seen better days.'

'You want us to hold him we catch up to him?'

'Be obliged if you can, Captain Edwards.'

'Not a problem.'

* * *

All the while, Johnny was taking a circuitous route far outside the town boundaries in an attempt to make his way through the pass unseen. By mid afternoon he was climbing through the forested foothills and, by switching ponies, he was making good headway.

At around the same time the sheriff had just managed to form and deputize a posse. Mayhew split his posse, three men under his deputy taking the road back towards Duzacres in case Johnny had headed that way, the remaining four following him towards the mountains where the captain and his troopers were already ahead of him.

Johnny's arm ached from the dragging pull of the lead rein from off the following pony and, as he climbed higher along the broad wagon trail, the colder air began to bite. He was thankful that he had not had to make the journey in the winter but, even though it was spring now, there was still snow on the peaks and the craggy grey rocks he rode past seemed to emit a chilling air. He shivered in his thin protection and clasped his arms around himself as he climbed higher and a cold wind blew down towards him.

It was wonderful country and if Johnny had been in a different frame of mind he would have taken note of the valley below. There lay a broad lake surrounded by sloping forests of thick pine, the water so calm it reflected the clear blue sky above like a mirror. A hunting eagle swooped amongst the trees with a high-pitched keen and only the rattle of dislodged pebbles from his shod ponies echoed in the stillness. Johnny was most aware of his loneliness just then, the loss of his parents and the dispersal of his brothers left him bereft of family support and this only served to deepen his sense of isolation. And now the prospect of being hunted for a murder he had not committed weighed down heavily on him creating a hollow place of despair in his heart. He had little to cling on to except the hope that somewhere over the mountains was a place where he could get lost and leave all his troubles behind.

He heard the singing before he saw the singer. A loud bellowing: the sound of a man's voice free of restraint amidst the wildness where no other could hear him. Or so Johnny thought. The steep-sided rocky cut through which he rode bent at a right angle up ahead and it was from around this bend that the singing came. He saw the mounted figure ahead as he turned the bend, a buckskin-clad figure whom he recognized immediately. It was the man he had sold the watch to in the saloon at Crosstrees. The probable killer of Preacher Inx: Edgar Freemantle.

Johnny reined in quickly but it was too late. Freemantle turned in the saddle at the sound of the ponies' shoes on the stone path. His singing stilled instantly. The two studied each other a moment, then Freemantle called out, 'Well, well, if it ain't the young fellow with the gold watch. What you doing up here, boy?'

'Same as you,' answered Johnny evenly.

'Is that right? And just what might that be?'

'Lighting out from the law.'

The trapper guffawed loudly. 'The law! Why I ain't got no trouble with the law. Why'd you say that?'

He geed his horse back towards Johnny, keeping one hand free and close to the rifle scabbarded under his saddle.

'I know it was you, mister,' persisted Johnny. 'You crept up on us in the dark of night and slit the preacher's throat. You done it as sure as these mountains is made of stone.'

Freemantle shrugged. 'That's a mighty serious accusation, boy. Why should I do such a thing?'

'That I don't know, but the preacher came back from seeing you with fear in his eyes and no gold watch in his hand.'

Freemantle chuckled, the sound

echoing rustily around the stone walls of the cut. 'Well, true to say he certainly left that saloon with his tail 'tween his legs.' His face changed suddenly as he neared Johnny; it was as if an icy wind had blown and pinched his features shut. 'Damned preachifier, he laid a curse on me. An evil curse. I don't like that; no man should do such a thing. Makes my skin feel all itchy and uncomfortable.'

'Makes me feel uncomfortable too, mister. Cos right now they'll be thinking I'm the one took his life. You got me to be a hunted man and that's the truth.'

Freemantle pulled up alongside Johnny, a smile creeping across his lips. 'That a fact? You mean to say you're a wanted man. There'll be a bounty on you, then.'

Johnny shrugged. 'That I don't know. I hid the body so no one'll know until it's found, if ever.'

The trapper scrubbed his unshaven chin with his fingers. 'No body, huh? That was smart, boy. Real smart.' He continued to eye Johnny thoughtfully. 'You the runaway?'

Johnny nodded.

'You didn't like him none then? This preacher, he your pa?' Freemantle asked.

'Nope, I didn't like him and he ain't my pa.'

'So, you're better off without him then, I guess?'

'It's true,' agreed Johnny. 'I am but I didn't wish him dead for all that.'

Freemantle's eyes shone with sly speculation, 'So you may say, young fellow, but might be no one else will believe you.'

'That's just why I'm on this here road.'

The trapper laughed suddenly, 'I like you boy. I like your style.' He stuck out a meaty paw. 'Edgar Freemantle's the name. Put it there.'

Tentatively, Johnny took the offered hand. 'Johnny Dollar,' he introduced himself, reckoning he had better continue with his pseudonym from now on.

‘These your ponies?’ Freemantle asked, looking the mounts up and down with an appraising eye.

‘I stole ’em. They’re the preacher’s’

Freemantle guffawed again. ‘Boy, you are a peach. Come on, Johnny Dollar, we’ll ride a ways together. Reckon you’ll be entertaining company.’

Johnny did not like the idea but he saw no other alternative than to accompany the trapper. They were both on the same road and he had no option to turn back. There was also the vague notion in the back of his mind that somehow he might be able to prove his innocence if he stuck close to the true killer of Preacher Inx.

They descended again and the view opened out as they entered a broad valley with the road ahead plain to see snaking its way through the valley slopes. Freemantle rode easily, sitting back in the saddle as easy as if he were in an armchair, his eyes glazed as if half-asleep. They rode in silence for a while until Johnny felt he had to ask.

'Why you so afeared of that curse Preacher Inx laid on you?'

Freemantle jolted from his muse. 'A curse is a terrible thing, Johnny Dollar. I lived with the Indians a spell. I seen what a spirit talker can do. It's real, believe me; you lay the bad word on a body and it sets in to lay you low. I known men drop down dead when a shaman blow pollen dust in their eyes. I watched women break out in a rash of bleeding spots when they find a devil doll in their tepee.' He shivered and it was not the cold. 'No human way of fighting it. It's a magic thing, way outside our understanding.'

'Is that why you cut the preacher?'

Freemantle frowned. 'He cussed me real bad. From now and for ever. If I'd let him live, I'd been dead within a sixmonth. 'T'weren't no other way. I had to cut the words from him.'

'You must've seen me, tied to that tree.'

'I saw you, Johnny boy.'

'You left me tied there. Why'd you do that?'

'None of my business, I guess.'

'What? You thought I tied myself up.'

'Gave no thought to it at all.'

Johnny shot the man a questioning sidelong glance. He saw it was no use pursuing the subject as Freemantle had already sunk back into his dreamy state again. An odd fellow, Johnny thought; a murderous cutthroat with a tender nervousness when it came to things of the occult. The world, Johnny concluded, is a strange place all right.

8

The half-breed watched them from amongst the closed clumps of spruce and pine on the hillside. He had taken an old Indian fishing trail alongside the lake. An unseen short cut unknown by the whites, it had brought him ahead of the two he now looked down upon from amongst the thick shadows under the trees.

Joseph Two Ponies was a half-breed Indian army scout, born of a white mother and a Cheyenne sub-chief. His mother had been abducted by the Cheyenne when she was a young girl on the verge of her teens; a raiding party on the hunt for livestock overran the newly built family homestead, killing the adults and carrying the youngster off. As with so many other tribes, it had been a traditional and practical abduction, the Indians needing women to bear their children, the young progeny to be trained as warriors, so it was often the case that they captured the young on their raids and adopted them into the tribe. It was a big country and a hard, dangerous life for the nomadic Indians. Only their numbers guaranteed their survival on the vast tracks of the open plains.

Joseph's mother had forgotten much of her childhood over the years, remembering little of her origins or the obstinacy of her father in his resolution to build a home on Cheyenne lands despite the many warnings he had received not to do so. Once she had reached maturity and been taken as one of the wives of the chief, Holding Bear, she settled contentedly into the life and, knowing no other, became virtually just another Cheyenne squaw. The two things she had retained, though, were her father's obstinacy and her native tongue. Both of these she had passed on to her son Joseph.

The troopers at the fort with their

predilection for nicknames, had taken to calling him Joey Tuppence, being unable to miss out on some corruption of his Indian name. It was really only an abbreviation indicating affection rather than any intended slight on his origins, and Joseph took it in the spirit intended, accepted the new name without any sense of offence. He liked the troopers anyway. The closed society of army life on a frontier fort encouraged a bond between rough men often placed in situations where they were reliant upon each other just to stay alive. Many of the troopers were untutored and undernourished immigrants of Irish or German origin, coming from poor backgrounds, and were only too glad to take on the dangers of army life for the benefits of a roof and regular meals, simple men who accepted the trials of each day as it came with little thought of the future.

Joey Tuppence found he liked the life and whilst he might find the occasional malcontent who would pass some critical observation on his heritage, the man was soon reprimanded by his barracks companions and Joey's status retained. Also, he was good at what he did. All the training he had received whilst amongst the tepees of the Cheyenne stood him in good stead as a tracker and scout, and with such experience he felt no distress in the lone situations in which he was often placed, as now, alone and far out in front of the supporting troop.

He mounted his pony and began to move out at a leisurely pace from the cover of the trees and down towards the road. As he went he slid the Winchester from its scabbard and placed it across his lap; he unbuttoned the flap on the army issue Navy Colt revolver and left it loose.

Joey Tuppence wore little indication of his Indian origins. He was dressed in a black round-topped crown hat with a wide brim, a dark jacket and cavalry pants. The only signatures he carried were the bead necklace and medicine pouch given to him by his father and a pair of moccasins hand-made for him by his mother. He rode slowly down the hillside until he reached the road, then he straddled it, waiting patiently for the two riders to come up to him.

'What's this?' muttered Freemantle, jerking into awareness as his sleepy eyes spotted the figure ahead.

Johnny squinted. 'Trouble, you think?'

'I don't rightly know.' Freemantle's head swivelled, eyes scanning the surrounding slopes. 'Lot of cover here. Best keep your wits about you.'

'Road agents?'

'More likely Indians. You see his moccasins. You armed, Johnny Dollar?'

'All I got is this here pocket knife.'

Freemantle barked a dismissive laugh. 'Oh, boy. You are a one. Indeed you are. Stay close, Johnny boy, we might need to make a run for it.'

They neared the lone figure and Freemantle pulled up when they were some forty feet apart.

'Howdy, there,' he called. 'Fine day,

wouldn't you say?'

Joey Tuppence sat straddling the road, side on, and silently watched them.

'Savvy English?' asked Freemantle, wondering at the fellow's refusal to answer.

Joey smiled. 'Oh yeah, I savvy English.'

'What you want, friend? You going to give us the road or we got to go around you?'

Joey raised his Winchester, crooked it over his bent forearm and cocked back the firing pin with a loud click. 'Mister, I'd like to see you keep your hands clear and for you both to dismount right now.'

Freemantle breathed deeply. 'Now, why'd we want to do that? You have something in mind?'

'My name is Joey Tuppence. I'm scout for the cavalry troop that's heading up the pass behind you. The sheriff down in Crosstrees has issued a warrant on this young man here and I aim to hold you both until my command catches up. So, do like I say and we won't have no trouble.'

Freemantle scratched his chin and glanced up at the forested slopes around them. 'You mean to say you're up here all on your lonesome and you feel the need to arrest two passing strangers. You ain't got the right, cavalry scout, or whatever you is.'

'Listen, mister,' Joey said coldly. 'I'll blow you off that saddle you don't get down right now.'

'All right, all right,' Freemantle looked down the menacing rifle barrel and shrugged obsequiously as he unhooked his foot from the stirrup. 'I'm going, I'm going. Best do like the man say, Johnny. He's the one with the gun.'

When the two were down, Joey Tuppence, keeping his rifle levelled, used his knees to guide his pony towards them. 'That's it,' he said. 'Keep your hands high.'

'Look here, 'breed,' Freemantle said, a little spitefully. 'You want to hold this boy, that's one thing. But there ain't no warrant out on me.'

'You're travelling together,' Joey answered. 'We'll see what the captain says. He says it's OK, then you can go your way. Right now though, you set and wait.' He waved the rifle at the roadside, bidding them to sit.

Obediently, the two sat crosslegged as Joey watched them, looking down from horseback, not he, his pony nor his Winchester wavering. They stayed that way for fifteen minutes, without a word being spoken, then Freemantle cleared his throat.

'Say, fella. You mind if I reach for a chaw of baccy? It's here inside my shirt.'

'Long as that's all that comes out.'

Freemantle felt down the neck of his buckskin and brought out a leather sack attached to a loop around his neck. He fumbled inside the pouch and took out a wad of chewing tobacco, broke of a piece and wedged it between his lip and yellowed teeth.

'Obliged,' he mumbled. 'Care for a

chaw?' he asked, offering the wad towards the scout.

Joey shook his head negatively, keeping his eyes firmly fixed on the man.

'How about you, Johnny?'

'No, sir. Thank you.'

Freemantle chewed enthusiastically as he fumbled to replace the wad in his pouch. 'That's real fine,' he mumbled, spitting a stream of juice into the road dust. 'Can't beat setting down in the wild woods with a pleasant chaw.'

The small-bore bullet took Joey Tuppence under the jaw. It lifted his head backwards and threw him from his saddle, the pony skittering away in a cloud of dust as the scout tumbled, to lie still on the ground. Johnny looked around in shocked surprise as the single shot echoed around the valley. Freemantle gave him a glance of wry satisfaction and held up the still smoking small twin-barrelled pearl-handled derringer he had slipped unseen from his tobacco pouch.

'Only takes one, Johnny boy. Long as you place it just right.' He rose easily to his feet, holding the derringer before him as he smacked Joey's restless pony away and bent over the body. 'Looks like he's still breathing,' observed Freemantle. 'Some of these half-breeds are certainly tough old boys.'

'Wh-why did you do that?' gasped Johnny.

'Only way, old sport. Neither of us want an unnecessary meeting with the sheriff back at Crosstrees, now do we?'

'No, but . . . ' Johnny was breathless, the suddenness and ruthless attitude of the trapper shocked him. 'Did you have to shoot him?'

Freemantle shrugged. 'He'd have done the same to us, I'll warrant.'

The trapper pointed his derringer and aimed a finishing shot at the unconscious scout's forehead. 'Best make sure,' he said. 'Then we'll be on our way.'

The rumble of approaching hoofs stayed his hand and he looked up quickly at the road behind. There, pennant flying, the scout's troop of cavalry was pouring down the track towards them, dust rising in a white cloud behind.

'Oh, Lord!' groaned Freemantle, shedding the derringer. 'Mount up and let's get going, Johnny boy.'

Both of them grabbed at their pony's trailing reins and swung themselves into the saddle. A warning shot from a carbine cracked out, the bullet smacking the air as it passed between them.

Freemantle sucked air through his teeth and pulled up, raising his hands high in the air. 'Best do the same, Johnny Dollar. I'm guessing those bluecoats are mean shots.'

Johnny looked at him accusingly as he accepted the inevitable and raised his hands as well.

The troop pounded up in a flurry of dust and troopers with levelled carbines soon surrounded the two.

'Sergeant, take a look at the scout,

will you,' Captain Loren Edwards ordered.

A burly trooper with chevrons on his arm dismounted and knelt over Joey Tuppence. 'He's out cold, Captain. Took a slug in the jaw by the look of it. It's busted all right but he ain't dead.'

Captain Edwards looked coldly at his two prisoners. 'You two abominations are lucky there. Which of you fired the shot?'

Freemantle shrugged. 'Look, Captain, this Indian here stopped us at rifle point on the road whilst we're going about our lawful business. We didn't know he was army, we thought he was just some two-bit thief, is all.'

'What?' snapped Edwards, pointing at the fallen scout's pants. 'You think those stripes on his legs mean nothing?'

'Hell, Captain, any Indian with half a head will wear the tunic pants off a fallen trooper. That don't mean a thing.'

Edwards curled a lip in distaste and turned his attention to Johnny. 'And what have you to say for yourself, young man. You're the runaway the sheriff's after for killing a man, aren't you?'

Johnny said nothing; shrivelled by the attention he just nodded vaguely, his eyes downcast.

'A pair of no-account murderers.' Edwards spat in disgust. 'Well, you two are going back to Crosstrees under guard. We'll leave you to the sheriff's tender mercies, although personally I'd like to string you both up right here and now.'

'What about Joey, sir?' asked the sergeant, raising the dazed scout's head on his bent knee. 'He needs some doctoring.'

The captain nodded. 'He'd best go back with them. Detail off four men, Sergeant. They'll escort the prisoners and see Joey gets medical treatment then follow us on to the fort. Wait on it a moment, I'll give the men a script to hand over.'

Edwards dismounted. He took paper and a pencil from his map case and began to write out a swift account of what had happened for the troopers to take back to the sheriff. He folded the sheet, gave it to one of the men and remounted as Joey Tuppence was loaded unsteadily on to his pony.

'Right, head back now, men. If you meet the sheriff's posse on the way, hand over the prisoners with that note and see they take care of Joey here. Then follow us on. No lingering in the town, we're needed up at Fort Bendix urgent, so you hurry after us. Understood?'

9

Gomar penitentiary was a newly built prison complex covering twenty-five acres. The main prison block housed forty-two stone built cells and was occupied by twenty-three prisoners at the time that Johnny and Freemantle arrived. Both had been sentenced to serve the usual harsh time issued in the day. Freemantle to three years' hard labour for his attack on Joey Tuppence. If it had been a white man he would have received more than double that.

Johnny, though, had a tougher time of it, his sentence for the alleged murder of Preacher Inx coming down as life with hard labour. He would have received the death sentence if it could have been proved beyond doubt that he was the assassin. As it was, he was the last person to have been seen with Inx and on a circumstantial basis he received life. Both their sentences were to be carried out at the Gomar pen.

They arrived ankle-chained together, as Sheriff Mayhew only had the one set, which he was very keen to see returned. They were brought in by the barred prison van, which carried them from Crosstrees. The simmering-hot day was overcast, which only added to the bleakness of the place as they stumbled down on to the prison yard. No walls had yet been built to enclose the prison, so it looked out over a cleared flat valley floor with only the scattered remains of skeletal tree stumps rising from the white dust. Surrounded by mountains, the prison stewed in trapped heat and the rugged range around them provided a natural barrier around the limestone quarries where the prisoners daily worked out their time.

'You men've been sent here to serve your time,' piped the superintendent rather obviously. He believed in making things transparently clear at the beginning, as often the charges who arrived into his care were either too dense, uneducated or badly beaten to understand what was happening to them.

'My name is Superintendent Blackmoore and you men are in my charge until your sentence is done.' He was a tall, gaunt and dour-featured man with deep sideburns, who had seen some harrowing army service as an officer during the Indian wars, and those days had left their mark on him. A perpetual tick flickered across one eye and he inadvertently tightened the muscles in his jaw continually as he nervously pressed his molars together. A haunted figure in a long funereal drape coat and stovepipe hat, he glowered at the two before him. A flowing white handkerchief was draped from one sleeve and he used this to wipe at his sweating brow occasionally.

'You'll receive a prison tunic,' he continued in his high voice. 'And a number. No names here, only numbers. Boss Lassiter?' He turned to the head guard standing next to him. 'What numbers have we now?'

Lassiter, a greasy, unshaven ox of a fat man with a bullwhip strapped to his gunbelt, studied a sheet.

'We have an 846 and 847 next, sir.'

'There you have it. Then you,' he pointed at Freemantle. 'Are 846 from now on. Freemantle, what are you here for?' He paused, studying Freemantle's charge over Lassiter's shoulder. 'Three years for assault and wounding with a firearm. Seems remarkably lenient. What did you do, 846?'

Freemantle shrugged. 'Shot an Indian, is all.'

Blackmoore looked surprised, his eyes widened as his own past experiences welled up in his memory. 'You shot an Indian and they gave you hard labour! Good grief! I would have thought they would have given you a bounty for such work. Anybody that rids us of that vermin deserves better than prison. Can't see what our legal system is coming to.'

'He was a 'breed army scout,'

Freemantle explained.

'Ah, I see,' The superintendent sighed knowingly. 'A half-caste with military friends at court, no doubt. Unfortunate, 846, but the law must be enforced wherever our own sympathies might lie.'

It was obvious he was viewing Freemantle's crime with a sympathetic eye as he mopped his brow and continued to study the sheet. 'And you, the young man with the life sentence, you are number 847. I hope the system is clear. Do you both understand?'

Freemantle, who had sunk into his meditative mood was staring deceptively vaguely at the mountains rising high behind them. He ignored the question. Johnny meanwhile stared disconsolately down at his feet.

'You hear me?' the superintendent snarled irritably. 'Wake them up, Lassiter.'

Boss Lassiter unrolled the bullwhip and snaked it out on the dusty yard, before snapping it in the air with a loud whistling crack.

'You heard the superintendent, boys,' he bawled. 'Now when he says 'd'you understand?' you give him quick and respectful answer or I'll flay your backs raw.'

'It's two to a cell in there,' Blackmoore continued coldly, indicating the prison building behind him with a loose wave of his handkerchief. 'You get out only to go to work. Honest work. Hard work that'll be the making of you, 846 and 847. It will set aside any notions you might have about continuing with the cruel deeds you have committed in your life before coming here. You, 847, will have a lifetime to consider your sinful act and you will think on it with repentance, I trust.' He nodded his head slowly, the top hat inclining as he did so. 'Now, Lassiter, take them to collect their prison garb. We have any trouble from either of you and it's a ball and chain, or bread and water and a spell in the solitary cell. Believe me, you won't like any of it. So behave, do as you're told and we'll all get along just fine. See them off, Boss Lassiter.'

The woollen tunic and pants they were given by the storeroom trusty were white with black bars looping them; a small tight-fitting cap was included as headgear. Their chains were removed and they were told to strip; their belongings, such as they had, were stored away as they dressed in their new clothes. As they went about this, Lassiter watched them keenly; trying to discover which of them might give him and his guards any trouble. He was a fat man, appearing slow and lethargic, yet his fat was hard and he could move with snakelike speed when necessary. He leant against the stone built wall as they changed, a match stuck between his teeth, his eyes hooded by a battered wide-brimmed hat.

'You boys got to understand something,' he said quietly, his voice full of menace as the two turned to look at him. 'Never mind about that undertaker Blackmoore out there, he's just for show. I'm the one who really runs things around here. You cross me, either of you, and you won't be waking up next morning, and that's a fact.'

Suddenly he moved away from the wall and struck Johnny hard along the side of the head with the handle of his bullwhip, which was made from a rolled steel grip beneath the leather. Johnny, taken by surprise, dropped to his knees, his head full of stars.

'Why'd you do that?' Johnny frowned up at him, rubbing his temple.

Boss Lassiter smiled easily as he leant back again. 'Cos I felt like it, fish.'

Freemantle nodded, helping Johnny to his feet. 'We got the message, boss,' he said. 'You won't have no trouble with us.'

'Be sure I don't. Going to enjoy having you boys here, it'll be like one long picnic, huh?' He chuckled wheezily and nodded at a day guard who stood grinning, a double-barrelled shotgun held slanted over the crook of his arm. 'Lock 'em down,' he ordered. 'They start work tomorrow.'

Freemantle paced their cell nervously. He counted out the steps as he marched the length of the stone floor, muttering to himself. Johnny lay on his pallet bed, rubbing his aching head and watching the trapper, who seemed to be in a high state of anxiety.

'What in heaven's name is it?' he asked at last.

Freemantle stopped his pacing and glared at him. 'It's a box, that's what it is.'

'A box?' Johnny asked bemused.

Freemantle waved his arms wildly at the cell walls. 'Here, this, it's a box.'

Johnny glanced around at the three stone walls and barred fourth and shrugged. 'Sure. Yeah, I guess it is, all right.'

'It's coming true,' mumbled Freemantle sadly, his arms dropping and hanging limply by his side.

'What is?' asked Johnny.

Freemantle looked across at him. 'I seen this mojo woman once. Down in Louisiana. Some old black witch with the second sight. She read the bones for me and foretold it. Said I'd end my days in a box.'

Johnny smiled at him wryly. 'We all do that, mister. Nothing new in that idea.'

'You don't understand. Not no pine box, boy. A box of stone and iron that would squeeze the breath from my body, she said. Like this here stone-walled cell with its iron bar door.'

Johnny looked across at the floor to ceiling thick iron bars, which separated them from the corridor outside and the other cells, which faced each other across the gloomy passageway. He remembered Freemantle's superstitious nature and how it had ultimately been the cause of the present troubles for both of them.

'Them's just words,' he said. 'Don't signify nothing.'

Freemantle whirled on him angrily. 'Maybe to you. But to me . . . ' he paused, looking away up to the single small barred window set high in the wall, 'they're the prospect of an end I don't care to think on just yet awhile.'

He sat down heavily on his own bunk, clutching his fists to his chest. 'I feel it starting already,' he gasped. 'I feel the breath being drawn out of me a parcel at a time.'

Johnny shook his head. 'Don't pay that no heed. It's in your head; there ain't no way a stone wall can take your breath away.'

'I'm a goner,' sighed Freemantle hopelessly.

Johnny could see there was no way of encouraging the trapper out of his despair. It was surprising to him that such an apparently tough and hardened creature could fade away for fear of a casual curse or gypsy prophecy. He learnt in that moment that a man can be governed all too easily by his beliefs and that only an ability to stand aside and be objective will allow a clearer perspective. We all are, Johnny considered then, our own worst enemies.

His thoughts were interrupted as the

cell house doors crashed open, the reinforced iron swinging back noisily, and a train of dusty prisoners filed in. Guards opened up the separate cells, the prisoners were ushered in and the bar doors locked behind them.

'Ho! Lookee here,' came a jeering cry. 'We got new fish.'

Tired eyes, in faces ghostly pale with white dust, turned in the direction of Johnny and Freemantle.

'Welcome to the Territory's outhouse,' called another. 'How come you made it in here?'

Johnny got up and grasped the bars. 'Howdy, you all. I'm Johnny Dollar and this here is Edgar Freemantle.'

'Only numbers in here, Fish,' came the answer from out of the gloom.

'OK,' mumbled Johnny. 'I'm 847, he's 846.'

'What time you got to do, boy?' asked an old man in the cell opposite.

'Me? I got to do the whole deal. My partner here is set for three years' hard.'

The old man crinkled his eyes and

took a long look at Johnny. He was a stringy fellow; his neck long and thin inside his tunic collar. The seamed and leathery skin seemed to have shrunk over his body and it appeared as if every muscle and tendon was raised and moved like mobile worms. His hair was thick and white as was his beard, although it may have been from the dust that coated his body.

'You got life, boy?' he said, rubbing at his face. 'That's a killing time for a young feller.'

'Reckon it's going to be,' agreed Johnny.

'What's the matter with your bud, there?' he asked, indicating the sullen figure of Freemantle, still hunched over on his bed.

'He ain't feeling too well at the present,' Johnny excused.

'Hah,' the old man chuckled. 'You just got here; wait 'til tomorrow. That's when it starts for real.'

'What?' asked Johnny.

'The quarry work, son. Man, that is

going to break you down, I tell you. You see the rest of these lowlifes in here?' he asked loudly, his hoarse voice calling into the darkness. 'Normally they're filled with the ginger of life. Look at 'em now. They's all beat an' run out, and that's a fact.'

A chorus of catcalls answered from the gloom. 'Shut your mouth, old man.'

'Go to hell!' the old man answered with a wry smile. 'What you gonna do, you bunch of no-accounts. Climb through them bars and shut me up. I'll say it as it is, where and when I please.'

'You been here too long, you old goat,' came a call. 'Got more wind in your whistle than a deadbeat like you has a right to.'

'Scum.' The old man spat derisively into the corridor, then turned his attention back to Johnny.

'Name's Ezra Pike,' he introduced himself. 'You can call me 503.'

Johnny did the numbers. 'That's a long way down the line,' he said. 'How long you got to go?'

‘Same as you, son. I’m here ’til my string runs out.’

‘Is it really as bad as that in this place?’ Johnny asked quietly almost in a whisper.

The old man nodded. ‘Think on it. They has four guards daytime and two at night. That’s all it takes to keep us all locked down, that and poor food and hard labour. Works wonders, the regimen they got us on here.’

Johnny nodded. ‘That and a long bullwhip.’

‘You met him, huh? Don’t cross that one. Boss Lassiter is an unquiet man. He enjoys inflicting pain; it’s like a disease with him. He likes to see a man scream as if it’s food and drink to him. He’s laid many a poor boy in the ground, I know, I seen it and then dug the graves.’

Johnny shuddered at the thought.

‘Leave the boy alone,’ came a deep voice from the next cell, its occupant out of sight to Johnny. ‘He’ll find out soon enough.’

'I's just saying,' Pike mumbled. 'That there is Kite Masters, he's your neighbour. Number 777. He likes to think he's gonna fly away one day.'

Freemantle jumped up and was suddenly at the bars next to Johnny. '777! You got a 777 in here? Man, that is one lucky number. Like to have your number, fellow.'

Freemantle pressed his face hard up against the bars, trying to see round the wall that divided them.

A deep laugh rumbled from the adjoining cell. 'You can have my old number any day you want, partner. Long as I get to leave it behind and I'm out of here for good.'

'Oh, I wish,' hissed Freemantle. 'I wish I had that number.' He turned to see Pike staring at him curiously from across the corridor. 'What you looking at, you bag of bones?' Freemantle barked angrily. 'Don't you go staring at me, you hear?'

The old man shrugged and brushed idly at the dust on his sleeve. 'Nothing to me, mister. You think numbers make a whole lot of difference, that's your business, not mine.'

'Damned right it is. Tend to your own affairs.'

'I surely will,' Pike said, and retreated slowly into the shadows at the back of his cell.

10

Over the next few months Johnny and Freemantle learnt the taste of the dust they had seen on the others that first evening. From early morning the loud rattle of batons on the bars and the cursing calls of the guards raised them from their bunks. A hurried and meagre breakfast was followed by a roll call on the prison yard before they were issued with pickaxes, steel chisels and long-handled hammers. Then they were marched off to the quarries. Cell partners were ankle-chained, one to the other, to frustrate any attempt at escape.

The guards who accompanied them rode horseback and carried Winchesters, holding the rifles in constant readiness. It was a long, hobbling march, the file of men being unable to stride out normally as the chains restricted them all to a shuffling gait.

The quarries were a bleak picture of raw white rock, split and hewn, the sides reaching high in vertical walls. A narrow-gauge track ran over the valley floor, with a large-wheeled metal trolley set on it to carry the mined ore. The prisoners tapped out cavities in line along a ledge, then they inserted a long steel wedge, which was hammered until a portion of rock cracked away under the beating and slid to the valley floor. There it was broken again into smaller pieces and loaded on to the trolley, to be moved to a wagon pick-up point and from there transported on to a crushing plant.

The pick-up point stood below a cliff edge, so that the trolley, on reaching the end of its sloping downhill run, would tip over and drop the raw ore into the waiting wagon. It was hot, dry work under a beating sun and the dust seemed to find its way into every orifice, clogging nostrils and pores alike. There was a constant need for water and Johnny, as the youngest, was detailed off to be water carrier. Unchained from Freemantle, he carried a bucket and ladle amongst the men, dispensing water when called for, which was often. This though, allowed Johnny to make contact with the other prisoners as he scampered and climbed around the quarry. In such a manner he was able to whisper a few words to his neighbour Kite Masters, the man with the lucky number 777.

Kite Masters was a giant of man, brawny and quiet. He moved with a gentle grace despite his height, which was well over six feet. He wore his fair hair long and it cascaded down his back in almost Indian fashion. Kite wielded the long handled-hammer easily and broke rock steadily on the quarry floor. He stood stripped to the waist, his muscles bulging under their sheen of sweat and dust as he swung in a steady rhythm.

His partner on the chain was a sickly looking fellow numbered 701, who obviously had difficulty with the work. He always stooped unsteadily in a crabbed position, picking up the broken rock and loading it into a basket before both he and Kite transferred the load into the trolley. He was wracked by coughs, blood was often on his lips, and there was no doubt that the cloud of dust that filled the air did little for his worsening chest condition.

'Your partner don't look too well,' observed Johnny as he served Kite a ladle of water, Kite's partner being out of earshot at the far end of the chain that linked them.

Kite nodded, his eyes hooded as he looked at Johnny. 'That's a fact, new fish.'

'Johnny Dollar, 847. We're neighbours.'

Kite harrumphed. 'Yep. Real homey ain't it?'

'Your partner should be up at the hospital.'

Kite cracked a solemn grin. 'Hospital? Sure enough they got a doctor here but he ain't worth a plugged nickel. Just a whiskey-loaded old soak. You get under his care and you won't make it through the first night. Nope, old 701 is better off here with me. I take good care of him best I can.'

Johnny heard a call for his attention and turned to leave. 'Nice meeting you,' he said in parting.

Kite raised the hammer, swung it over his head and brought it down with a thunderous crack. 'Get out now if you can, Johnny Dollar,' he said as the rock at his feet split apart.

'What d'you mean?' asked Johnny, turning back.

'Whilst you're still strong,' muttered Kite, lifting the hammer again. 'This place will break you down so you can't lift one foot over the other you wait long enough. No way you can run after that.'

Run! It was the first time Johnny had even considered the notion of escape. Despite his innocence of the crime, like so many uneducated young men in similar positions he had accepted the lot handed down to him by the authorities without question, as a due process of law to be borne without complaint. To escape was a new concept, which entered into his untutored mind like a sudden bright light. Indeed, it was true. He could run. He was young and fit; the prospect of a life term, which he had, at first accepted as inevitable suddenly took on a different perspective. Johnny began to look at the quarry in a new light.

'What'd he say?' asked Freemantle, as Johnny gave him water.

'Who?' asked Johnny.

'Why, lucky 777, of course. Who else?'

'He said I should get out whilst I'm still able.'

Freemantle looked speculatively across at Kite. 'He did, did he? That's real interesting. Might be he's planning something himself.'

'Aw, I don't know. It was just an observation, I reckon.'

Freemantle shook his head. 'He's lucky. He's got the fortune with him. I'd like to be alongside him if he makes a break. Get out afore this place chokes the life out of me.'

'He didn't say nothing about any escape. 'Sides, he's locked on to that poor fellow 701, who don't look like he's got much more in him.'

'He don't have to say nothing about escape out loud, boy. It's the kind of thing you only whisper around here. Stay close. You hear something, you tell me, huh?'

Johnny nodded doubtfully. 'Sure thing.'

* * *

Ezra Pike began his prattle that night without preamble. It was a regular session and his noise irritated everybody in the cellblock. Ezra had no companion in his cell to annoy, he was the odd number in the prison line-up and being the oldest resident, was considered the safest to leave unchained. But his tongue wagged continually and only his simpering closeness to the guards had kept him alive this long. It was considered by many that his favouritism by the guards indicated an unhealthy status amongst the prison population and that he probably reported regularly back to the superintendent.

Pike worked in the infirmary or about the storeroom three days a week and three days in the quarry. This, plus the day off for Sunday, allowed him an easier regime than any other prisoner and was considered by all to be a pay-off for his spying.

'How're enjoying your first few weeks here, 847?' he called across to Johnny, after supper and the nightly lock-down.

Johnny raised his tired head. 'Just fine,' he answered.

'*Just fine*!' guffawed the old man. 'You hear that, the rest of you bums? The boy's doing 'just fine'. My, my! What are you on about, boy? There's nothing fine about this place.'

'I meant, I'm surviving, I guess.'

'Uhuh,' nodded Pike. 'Guess we're all doing that. Just about. How about you, 701?' he called over towards Kite's cell. 'You surviving? How's that cough of yourn, any better?'

Everybody recognized the needling tone and Johnny knew by now that the old man took delight in fomenting trouble from the safety of his favoured position.

'Watch your mouth, 503,' Johnny heard Kite rumble dangerously.

'I's just asking,' said Pike innocently. 'You OK, Kite? Didn't mean nothing by it. Honest I didn't.'

'Just mind your business,' warned Kite.

'Sure, sure,' said the old man. 'How about it, water boy? Getting along with your neighbour, old Kite there?'

'It's fine. Like I said, just fine.'

'Only I seen you two are right pally now,' the old man needled. 'Visiting real nice over the water bucket the other day.'

'Don't know what you mean. I gives

water to them that's asks is all.'

'Yeah, but what's there to find to talk about here, 'cept dust and when you're getting out.'

'Well, I'm tired,' said Johnny, ignoring Pike's pestering. 'Going to get my head down now.'

'That's right, young fellow. You get your beauty sleep. Going to need it.'

'Why don't you just shut up!' bawled Freemantle, from where he thrashed on his sleepless bunk. 'You're worse than a papoose's rattle, the way you dribble on.'

'Wouldn't know about that, 846. I never bedded down with no Indians. Dirty folk, you ask me. Heard you spent some time with them, though.'

'Sure did, you leaking bucket. And they was a damn sight more peaceable than you are.'

Pike, not to be outdone, had to have the last word. 'Well, each to his own, I say. Each to his own. Be it crawling bedbugs or stinking Indians, it's all the same to me.'

When all was quiet Freemantle whispered across to Johnny. 'Watch that old man, Johnny boy. I'll warrant he's the telegraph line direct to Boss Lassiter and that's a fact.'

Johnny nodded in the darkness. 'I know it,' he agreed.

'One day I'll wring that scrawny neck given half a chance,' promised Freemantle with venom. 'You heard any more?' he asked.

'Not a peep,' Johnny answered honestly.

'Keep your ear to the ground then. Something's popping, I'm sure of it. And we want to be in on it when it happens.'

How Freemantle could know such a thing, Johnny had no idea. But Freemantle was a mysterious fellow, sensitive to the atmosphere and in touch with unseen waves of emotion that had no apparent reality amidst the stone cell walls. Johnny recognized that his trapper's skills of silent appraisal and patience stood him in good stead in the charged electricity of the prison environment and that he just had to taste the air to know that something was afoot.

11

When it happened it was at an unexpected moment. Only later did Johnny come to understand Kite's apparently benevolent attention to his sickly cellmate. It was all for this day.

'Man down here, boss!' came the call and Johnny turned to see Kite standing over the fallen body of his cell companion. Heads turned from all around the quarry workings as the call echoed off the quarry walls and one of the guards on horseback sidled slowly over.

'What's the problem?' asked the guard, looking down.

'I think he's a goner,' answered Kite, turning 701 on his side.

The guard began to dismount as he called over to his partner. 'Getting down here!'

'I got you,' answered the other guard, raising his rifle.

The first guard knelt and examined 701. 'Yeah, he's gone. We got a dead one here,' he shouted across, taking the shackle keys from his belt. He looked up at Kite. 'I'm going to undo you now, so you step back clear, you understand?'

'Yessir, boss,' said Kite, stepping away. 'He's been sick for a long while. He was about due to leave.'

'I see that,' said the guard, beginning to unlock the shackle from the dead man's ankle.

A wind blew up as the guard struggled with the rusted lock and it raised dust devils across the bleached quarry floor. Johnny felt a wave of tension run through him as he felt the hot wind and he turned slightly to see where Freemantle was working. The trapper was moving slowly away from his work site, making his way down towards the mounted guard, silently treading light footed through the bowling clouds of dust.

'Best get a wagon up here,' called the

kneeling guard, looking up. 'Pike, you here? 507, where are you? Damned old man, never there when you want him.'

'I'm here, boss, I'm here,' called Pike, coming out of the dust clouds. He shielded his eyes against the blowing dust and looked across at the mounted guard, making out Freemantle stealthily advancing on him.

'Best watch your back there, boss,' Pike warned. 'Prisoner on the move.'

The mounted guard whirled his pony around at the call, 'Keep your distance, 846. Or I'll blow your fool head off.'

Freemantle spread his arms wide, a steel wedge held loosely in one hand. 'Nothing, boss. Nothing. I'm just seeing what's up here, is all,' he said in a placating tone.

Then it happened quickly, in a blur of movement. The shackles fell from the dead man's ankle and Kite instantly drew the chain in, whipping it as easily as a lariat in his strong grip. He lashed it at the kneeling guard who gasped in dismay as the flying chain encircled his neck like a snake. The mounted guard heard his choking sob and turned back. At that moment Freemantle threw the heavy steel wedge as if it were a throwing knife. The nine-inch piece of metal whirled through the air with an audible hum and caught the guard hard on the back of the head. His hat flew off, high and, taken by the wind it scampered across the quarry. The guard weaved for a moment in the saddle, and then fell heavily to the ground.

'Get the ponies!' Kite called as he jerked the chain taut with a sudden movement. Men rushed forward to obey his command and took the two ponies by the reins. The guard at the chain end gurgled, his face turning purple. With brutal coldness Kite pulled savagely once more; the man jerked and slid to the ground. Kite knelt quickly beside him, took the keys from his fingers, and unlocked the shackle at his own ankle.

'You did that real nice,' praised Freemantle, running up, his victim's rifle in his hand.

'Not so bad yourself,' said Kite. He took the pistol from the guard's belt and thrust it into the top of his prison pants.

Prisoners were gathering with serious expressions on their faces. Johnny watched in dumb surprise, not sure of what to do amidst the silent tension and whipping wind. Quickly the two guards were stripped of their clothes and weapons and left lying in their longjohns.

'You shouldn't be doing this,' warned Pike. 'There'll be hell to pay.' His thin voice rising shakily over the wind.

Freemantle sneered and turned to face him, cocking the Winchester as he did so.

'No!' shouted Kite. 'Don't do it. The shot'll be heard at the prison.'

Fuming, Freemantle saw the sense in it and lowered the rifle. 'We've got to shut him up, he'll go tittle-tattle soon as he can.'

'I know it,' agreed Kite. He strode

over and grasped the old prisoner by the throat, raising him on to his toes. Johnny jerked out of his state of shock and ran over as he saw Kite's intention.

Already prisoners were making off at the run, some clad in vestiges of the guard's clothing. A hat here, a pair of pants, all oddments worn over their prison garments. There was a whirl of activity all around in the swirling white dust as prisoners mounted the ponies, two and three to a horse and rode off.

Johnny grabbed at Kite's muscled arm. 'No, don't,' he said. 'Enough killing. Leave him be.'

Kite looked down at Johnny through slitted eyes. Pike was held struggling at arm's length the massive fist locked around his throat. 'Has to be,' growled Kite.

'Enough,' said Johnny firmly. 'All said and done, he's one of us.'

Kite looked at him a long moment, then bunching his fist he delivered a mighty blow with his free hand. Pike's eyes rolled in his head as the blow rocked his jaw. Kite dropped the unconscious old man and turned to Johnny and Freemantle. 'Let's get out of here, then.'

'Where do we go?' asked Freemantle. 'The others took the horses.'

Kite grunted. 'I guess they forgot the ore wagon. Come on, we'll take that.'

Together they ran to the cliff edge at the trolley's rail end and saw the empty wagon standing below with a team of six tethered mules ready to pull.

'Here,' said Kite. 'I'll lower you both down.'

It was a steep drop of about eighteen feet. At arm's length they could just about manage the fall.

'How about you?' asked Johnny.

'I'm the tallest, I'll manage.'

Kite grasped Johnny's wrists and lowered him over. Lying flat, Kite spread his legs wide between the trolley rails for purchase. Johnny was surprised at the man's massive strength, still intact after years of prison diet and harsh labour. At full stretch and at the end of his reach, Kite let go and Johnny dropped safely down on to the plank bed of the wagon.

Kite was in the process of lowering Freemantle when they all heard a metallic rumble coming from the scudding dust behind.

'What's that?' shouted Johnny over the rising howl of the wind.

Dangling, Freemantle called out, 'It's the trolley. That damned old man's set it going on the rails.'

Kite let go of Freemantle and rose to his knees ready to jump aside. Caught unawares, Freemantle tumbled down, his leg twisting awkwardly under him as he landed heavily inside the wagon. The trapper howled in pain as his leg broke with an audible snap.

Pike had started the loaded trolley on its run down with vengeful energy, fuelled by his intense anger. He cursed them loudly, unseen from amidst the clouds of whirling dust, a scream almost as loud as the raging wind. Normally a brake man would control the trolley's run down the rails, but without such a slowing process the solid iron box gained momentum and with its full load of heavy rock it soon reached a speed equivalent to that of an oncoming train.

The trolley burst out of the clouds of dust and hit Kite full on as he was rising to his feet. The box, taking the body of Kite with it, crashed through the rail-end buffers and cartwheeled over the edge of the cliff with a screeching roar. Johnny looked directly up at the descending upended trolley with its piles of broken stone flying down towards him. Instinctively he leapt out of the wagon bed and rolled on to the ground away from the vehicle.

Freemantle had no chance; his shattered leg held him trapped in the wagon and the great trolley with its heavy load fell directly upon him. The wagon collapsed and was flattened under the massive impact; shattered pieces of timber and splintered rock flew in all directions. Johnny rolled away from the lethal column of dust and debris but still he was battered by rubble from the burst. The mule team screamed in fear and bucked, sashaying from side to side and straining to escape their traces, but they were held tight to a solid hitching post and could only complain loudly as the dust enveloped them.

As the dust settled, Johnny rose unsteadily to his feet. His heart was pounding loudly in his chest and he panted in shock at the sudden devastation. Numbly he made his way over to the remains of the wagon, which lay buried under the battered trolley and its load of rock.

'Edgar?' he whispered hopefully. But there was no sign from the trapper, who had surely met his end as foretold by the mojo woman in Louisiana, entombed in an iron and stone box with the breath crushed out of him. Johnny saw Kite's crumpled body lying nearby; he ran over to it but it was no use, the big man had been killed by the trolley's driving impact. Sadly, Johnny knelt beside him and with tightly compressed lips withdrew the pistol still held in Kite's prison pants. He searched around and found Freemantle's rifle lying coated in white dust. Idly he cleaned away the dust with his sleeve as he wondered what he should do now.

'Damned well served them right.' The spitting cry came from above and Johnny looked up to see the figure of the embittered Ezra Pike standing hunched at the brim of the drop. Blood ran from his lips where Kite had struck him. As the dust swirled about him Pike took on an almost demonic appearance, his hair and beard flying in the wind.

'Why'd you do it?' cried Johnny angrily. 'You killed them both.'

'Sure I did,' hissed Pike. 'And glad of it, that big'un near broke my jaw.'

Johnny raised his hand, the revolver pointing at the figure above. His arm shook with anger and the barrel quivered over its target.

'Don't even think on it,' called Pike smugly. 'They'll be coming from the prison now, I'll say you helped me.

Saved me from that lug Kite. There's nowhere else to go, boy. They'll be all over the Territory looking for runaways and when Boss Lassiter gets through with them their skin'll be in ribbons.'

Johnny fired then. Three shots that buckled the body of Pike. The old man's eyes opened wide in surprise and he tumbled forward with a keening cry, to drop down limply on to the bodies of the men he had killed so wantonly.

The shots raised Johnny from his stupor. He looked at the smoking pistol in his hand almost as if it were someone else who had fired the shots. Then, grimly he shook his head clear and turned towards the skittering mules.

It was time to run.

12

He kept on running for five long years.

Although he did not realize it, during that time Johnny Dollar had earned a name for himself. He started out fair enough, panhandling his way into cow camps and taking odd jobs in out of the way townships. At first fearful and forever looking over his shoulder for the shadow of Boss Lassiter he played a meek and subservient role. Eventually though, time wore off those nagging fears and Johnny assumed a more determined attitude, filled with the sense of freedom that his meanderings allowed. The capable characteristics that had been his during childhood returned to him, surely inherited traits from his determined but long dead father.

By the year 1887 Johnny had learnt to handle the six-gun and to shoot accurately with the rifle. He gained a job riding shotgun for the small Legget & Fox Stage line. Hardened and more brittle now, Johnny reached his twentieth year with a reasonably fast draw and a readiness to use it. But his life was one of constant restless movement, the dark memory of prison still imprinted on his mind as of a place he had no wish to return to. For this reason he stayed with the stage line, riding up on the box next to the hard-bitten old driver, Gunny Sack Debreau. In such a way Johnny kept on moving, never in one place for long enough to be noticed.

Gunny was a Confederate veteran and, much to the consternation of his passengers, who had enough trouble sleeping in the cramped and bouncing conditions of the Concord coach, would sing at tuneless top volume the Southern Army's most popular and depressing ballad, *Lorena*. An unrequited love song so sad that southern generals had tried to get it banned on the premise that it was bad for morale.

A verse or two of the melancholy song was enough to handle the beginning and end of the ten- to fifteen-mile trip between swing stations. The rendition always ended with Gunny's loud bawling call of 'Lorena!', intended part as a crescendo climax but also to advise the distant station attendant that a change of horses was due and to prepare accordingly. Johnny bore the repetition of the song in long-suffering silence; he liked the tough old driver, who had seen it all and survived more than one attack by Indians and outlaws, and in his affection he was prepared to be generous with the old-timer's foibles.

They rode the stage trail with regularity, taking the hundred-mile daily trip with practised ease, carrying mail and passengers where the railroad had not yet reached. This suited Johnny's liking for anonymity as they only hit on small towns and backwoods hamlets that lay along the full stageline route covering a total of 1,200 miles in all. But the railroad was coming and soon even this small stageline would be put out of business by faster and cheaper competition. Already the mighty Overland Stageline was gone and Legget & Fox only survived by serving the small margin left by their departure.

The sun was setting into a wide Wyoming sky fractured by orange and purple rainclouds as Gunny settled into the last verse, from which Johnny knew they were approaching the home station of Forty Rod where they could rest and get a meal. Gunny slapped the reins across the backs of the six-up team and hollered out the final few stanzas as the station came into sight.

There is a future, oh, thank God!
Of life this is so small a part
'Tis dust to dust beneath the sod
But there, up there, 'tis heart to heart.
. . . Lorena! . . .

Johnny and the passengers inside breathed a sigh of relief as Gunny caved in at last and fell silent.

'Man, I am hungry,' growled Gunny, hauling on the brake handle as they swung into the low, sod-walled station. 'Hope that old hoss has something good in the pot tonight.'

Johnny stretched to ease his back. He set his boot on the wheel rim, then the hub, and jumped lightly down. He poked his head into the coach's interior, where the passengers all sat huddled in company dusters against the cool night air and prairie dust, 'OK, folks, forty minute stopover. Hot food waiting inside, so get yourselves down.'

He, like Gunny, wore a high-collared buffalo hide overcoat against the cold. He shook it off as the passengers descended. It would be warm inside the station and after the wind-whipped journey he knew he would soon feel overheated inside the snug coat.

There were five passengers all told, two men and three women. None was exceptional in any way from the many passengers who passed through their hands. A married couple, Mr and Mrs Lowbank, returning to their home in Chrome City. Of the other two ladies, one was a very tall, horse-faced woman bound to join her husband, a private serving with the cavalry at Fort Havering. The other, a pretty young bookish girl, had an unknown reason for her journey but was bound for Julesville. The other male passenger, a silent young fellow wearing a sack jacket and long fair hair tucked up inside his roll-brimmed bowler, carried a doctor's holdall, so Johnny took him to be a medical man or huckster travelling on to the end of the line.

Johnny let Gunny guide the passengers in and stood idly watching whilst the liveryman and his young son unfastened the team. They took them off to the post corral standing next to a stone barn that ran at right angles to the more poorly constructed sod-walled station house. After the roar of the coach on the trail and Gunny's insistent serenading it was pleasant to listen to nothing but the distant rumbling of a passing storm far off on the otherwise silent prairie, and Johnny drew it in, letting the bucking ride ease out of his body.

'You take the evening air, conductor?' It was the young, bookish girl, coming up behind him. 'I would have thought you would have had enough of that already.'

Johnny politely touched the brim of his hat in recognition, a flat-brimmed, dark-coloured round-crowned sombrero he had just purchased and was very proud of.

He smiled. 'It's the silence I'm getting my fill of, ma'am. Old Gunny there can dent your eardrums some.'

The girl giggled lightly. 'He has a very strong voice, indeed,' she agreed.

Johnny looked her over, his gaze shaded by the approaching darkness. She was probably his own age with a handsome, heart-shaped face. Dark curly hair pressed energetically out from under her bonnet and she had a look in her grey eyes that he liked instantly. A steady, even look that did not fall away as he studied her.

'It is beautiful, isn't it?' she breathed, indicating the last rays of a hot, red sun as it descended through the departing rain clouds on the horizon and caught them in ribbons of bright gold.

'Sure is. Be cold later though.'

'I don't mind,' she said, hugging her arms about her. 'This is my first journey West. And I will enjoy every moment of it.'

Her voice was educated and well modulated but she spoke softly, as if confiding in him alone.

'You like it so far?' Johnny asked.

'Well, it's rough and ready, that is for sure, but still I like it. The scale of everything is so vast I feel I can breathe easy here. It's very bracing.'

'May I ask where you're from, ma'am?'

'Far away.' She laughed lightly. 'From

New York city. I'm taking a post as schoolteacher in a town called Julesville. You know it?'

'I do, ma'am. It's our changeover stop, where the new driver and guard take over. It has its nice parts.'

'Forgive me,' she said suddenly and held out her gloved hand. 'I'm Miss Joanna Moore.'

Johnny took off his hat and took her offered hand. It was so small that for a moment he feared he would grip her too tightly. 'Johnny Dollar.'

'Johnny Dollar.' She sighed as she repeated it. 'What a remarkable name.'

'Not so you'd notice, ma'am.'

'I'm sorry,' she said. 'I didn't mean to be rude. It's just that everything is so new to me. I'm a little too excited by my adventure, I fear.'

Johnny ducked his head shyly; he was not at all used to this personal attention by such a pretty young woman, and especially a city-educated one.

'I guess we'd better go on inside,' he said shyly. 'That old Gunny will have demolished half the feed laid out if we're not careful.'

'One moment more.' She laid her hand on his arm and Johnny almost shivered at the touch. 'You said Julesville had some nice parts. What did you quite mean by that?'

'Well there's a nice part of town and a not so nice part,' he answered obliquely.

'I'm sorry. I don't understand,' she confessed with a shake of her head.

'It's a coal-mining town. You get on the wrong side of Main Street and you're into the bawdy houses and saloons; things can get a little hectic. Best not be in a place you should avoid, if you can.'

A frown creased her brow, 'Oh, really . . . Well then, I see. Thank you for your advice, Mr Dollar.' She turned. 'Shall we go inside?'

The food was good. They all dined well on salmon and trout from a nearby stream, with helpings of buffalo-berry jelly to follow. Although the poor Mr

Lowbank had not taken Johnny's advice at the start of their journey and his oil-slicked hair had now taken on a coating of road dust more like adobe. For most of the meal he kept his head in a bucket of water, trying to loosen the cemented mix. His wife did little but smile calmly at his discomfort with a knowing look, as if well used to his blunders.

The tall female passenger, on her way to Fort Havering, was an agitated woman and giggled continually in a hypertensive way. Her horse face gave her the appearance of a braying pony as she giggled and exposed a fine set of buckteeth. She waxed lyrical and somewhat excessively about her soldier husband, advising proudly that, although her man was well below her own stature — almost a dwarf by comparison, she declared, he was a veritable tiger beneath the blanket and she could not wait to reacquaint herself with his company. A fact that those around the table agreed in silent accord, was private information which they could well have done without knowing.

After the meal a bottle of Valley Tan whiskey was passed around for the gentlemen. Joanna looked curiously at the pale brew as it was poured.

'A local liquor. How is it made all the way out here?' she asked.

Gunny took a swallow and slapped the bare planks of the wooden-topped table smartly with a loud, 'Hah!' He shook his head from side to side as the strong liquor bit. ' 'Tis made from horned toads and rattlesnake venom,' he answered, laughing across at her.

'Really?' Joanna asked innocently. 'That sounds truly disgusting.'

'No, my dear,' said Mrs Lowbank sitting opposite. 'He's just joshing you. But you are right in one thing, it is awful stuff. Distilled from wheat and potatoes, and a very fiery brew it is too.'

Johnny smiled as Joanna blushed slightly in embarrassment, and in an attempt to impress her he downed his glassful in one long swallow. A foolish move. It nearly gagged him, coursing a searing path on its way down his insides. 'Phew!' he breathed, almost speechless. 'That sure is a powerful mix.'

'Go on, Johnny boy,' chuckled Gunny, filling his glass. 'I could drive through the whole Sioux nation on a bottle of Valley Tan. Have another.'

They all sat facing each other along opposite sides of the dining table in the low roofed room. There was a fire burning in a brick grate at one end, and off to one side were the cooking and washing necessaries where Mr Low-bank still stood crouched over his bucket of water. The station manager, Acer Smith, scurried around them collecting tin plates and wiping down the bare-plank table top with a not too clean cloth. Candles and lamps burned dimly, giving the place a cosy feel and probably hiding the myriad of spider's webs and other signs of creatures that hid in the dark shadows of the ceiling.

'Mighty fine, Acer,' congratulated

Gunny warmly. 'Best damn fish I've had in a twelvemonth.'

'You're welcome to her, Gunny. The lad outside is good with the rod and catches up a netful near every day.'

Johnny looked down at his refilled glass, wondering how he was going to avoid drinking the powerful brew, when he noticed small quivering circles forming on the surface. He felt it then, a slight vibration under his boots through the earthen floor. 'Something's coming,' he said.

'I feel it,' Gunny agreed. 'Horses travelling fast.'

A fearful silence overtook the table as all the passenger froze and looked wide-eyed at one another, wondering what this meant. Johnny took out his pistol and laid it lightly on the table top as Gunny picked up the shotgun leaning against the wall behind him.

'What is it?' asked Joanna, staring at Johnny's gun. 'Wild savages?'

'Don't worry, folks,' said Acer Smith cheerfully. 'Put them firearms away, boys. It's only the Titan coming in, that's all.'

'The Titan?' said Gunny, frowning. 'She making a run tonight?'

Acer nodded. 'They're just here for a changeover. Be straight on out again, I'm sure. The Titan don't stop for nobody.'

'What is it, this Titan?' Joanna asked.

'It's a special from the Federal Mint,' Johnny obliged, sliding his pistol back in the holster. 'A reinforced steel-plate coach. They usually carry bullion. Has a big old strongbox bolted down inside. Manufacturers claim it'd take a long day to open that box up, it's so solidly made.'

'Believe it when I see it,' snorted Gunny doubtfully. 'Ain't nothing like gold eagles to make a fellow pop a strongbox, no matter how it's fixed.'

'Surely though,' said Joanna, 'it's truly a very tempting prize for any road agents?'

'Indeed it is,' agreed Johnny. 'But they have two guards alongside the driver and carry no passengers. The Titan goes straight through at speed. Unlike us, she drives day and night, twenty-four hours without a stop except for team change.'

The rumbling was getting louder now as the heavy vehicle approached the station, causing hanging pots to rattle over the fireplace and china to clatter on the shelves. They were all silent as the coach drew noisily into the station with much shouting from the driver for the liveryman to bring out the new team. Then there was only the sound of hard blowing, hoof-stamping horses, the rough call of impatient men and the jingle of loosened tackle.

The silent young man with the doctor's holdall casually raised it to his lap and unsnapped the fastener. Without a word he drew out a long barrelled silver plated Peacemaker. Then he rose from his seat.

'You folks all pay close attention now,' he said.

It was the first time he had spoken

and all eyes turned to him, widening as they saw the gun. He stepped to one side of the room, his back against the wall as he covered them all. Then he drew a second pistol from his deep jacket pocket. Another revolver, this one shortened, with the barrel cut down to two inches from the cylinder. The young man smiled thinly.

'You there, Conductor. Place that hog leg on the table. Use your left hand, real easy.' As Johnny obeyed, he watched the two pistols as they panned across the occupants of the room. 'Old-timer, don't even think about that shotgun and you, station manager, set yourself down. Feller with the bucket on his head, you'd better take a seat too.'

As Acer obeyed and Mr Lowbank nervously clutched a towel to his dripping hair, there was the sound of irritated shouting from outside. 'Hell, where's those horses? Come on, damn you, we ain't got all night.' The call was followed by a single loud rifle shot that made everybody jump, then a cacophony of firing broke out. Johnny watched the young man but he kept his eyes fixed firmly on them all without taking any notice of the gunfire outside. 'Just you all set steady,' he said, 'and no harm'll come to you.'

There was something vaguely familiar about the fellow but Johnny couldn't quite place where he'd seen him before. The shooting stopped as suddenly as it had started, then the door burst open and a portly man dressed dandily in a silver-buttoned Mexican jacket and striped pants entered. He wore a broad, roll-brimmed black hat canted to one side with a long, brightly patterned scarf over the lower part of his face. Under the shadow of his hat brim his eyes quickly took in the room. He glanced across at the young man.

'Everything OK?' he asked, as a tall gaunt man dressed in a long slicker and carrying a smoking rifle bustled in behind him.

The young man nodded. He said nothing but waved the silver-plated pistol-barrel in Johnny's direction. The man with the Mexican jacket gave Johnny a long, hard stare.

'What?' said Johnny. 'Do I know you fellows?'

Without answering, the Mexican jacket leant over and picked up Gunny's shotgun. 'All right,' he said. 'We're here for the Titan but I want you folks to spill your valuables on the table. There's a dead man outside and a wounded one too, so you will know we mean business. Act nice and all will be fine. Any trouble and we'll cut you down without an ounce of mercy.'

Nervously, the passengers complied, and dollar bills, coin, gold watches and purses were dropped on the table top, whilst the rifle-bearing gaunt-looking outlaw grinned toothlessly and scooped them into a central pile. Johnny watched as Joanna's fingers trembled, fumbling with the fastener on her reticule.

He leant over. 'Here,' he said. 'Let me.' As he took the bag and snapped it open, he whispered to her. 'Don't be afraid, all will be well.' She looked at him with troubled eyes and bit her lip nervously.

'I do hope so,' she whispered back.

The gaunt man reached up to snatch the bag from him, but Johnny stayed his hand by grasping his wrist and holding it tightly. The man looked up at Johnny, his lips compressing over his empty gums as he brought up the rifle still held in his other hand.

'Leave it be, Pete!' snapped the man in the Mexican jacket. 'I apologize for old Pete Medly, folks,' he went on. 'As you can see he ain't got a tooth in his head and not much else either.'

Pete grinned toothlessly at them all and obediently pulled back away from Johnny. Despite his grin, though, his eyes slitted and slid over Johnny in a predatory fashion.

When they were done, the Mexican jacket poked at the pile on the table with the end of the shotgun barrel. 'That's fine,' he said. 'Thank you all most kindly. Now I want you to make your way out to the barn there and join the liveryman and boy inside. We intend to lock you all away until we're done here. Perhaps you ladies will help out with that wounded guard; the Titan driver don't seem to be much of a doctoring sort.' He nodded at his gaunt companion, 'See 'em out, Pete.'

The ringing sound of heavy hammering was coming from outside now as the rest of the gang feverishly attacked the strongbox with hammer and chisel. As the party filed out, the Mexican jacket held up the shotgun barrel, stopping Johnny from leaving. 'You stay here,' he ordered.

When the three of them were alone Johnny asked, 'What's this about?'

In answer the portly fellow lowered his mask with a forefinger and the young man shed his bowler letting a wave of curly blond hair fall over his shoulders.

'Damn, Johnny,' said the Mexican jacket with a laugh. 'It's good to see you again.'

Johnny's jaw dropped as he recognized first one then the other. 'By all that's holy!'

'Yeah, Johnny, it's us. Adam and Billy,' said the young one with the golden locks. 'I didn't recognize you at first, you sure have changed some. I'm called Curly Bill now, cos of this.' He played the silver-plate gun barrel through his hair.

Johnny, even through his surprise, recognized the simple tones of his younger brother. 'How in hell . . . ?' he asked.

Adam tossed his hat on the table and poured himself a shot of the demonic whiskey. 'It's all your fault, brother,' he said.

'My fault!' gasped Johnny. 'How so?'

'Well, once you took off from that Preacher Inx and then cut him good when he caught up with you, the whole town was in a fever. You should've heard it, Johnny. That Widow Inx, weeping and greeting, the old witch had never had it so good, everybody falling all over her with pity. She let on they called you Johnny Dollar, after them wages you asked for. Then we heard you was sent up to Gomar pen after killing that army scout — '

'Wait a minute,' begged Johnny. 'I never killed Inx or that scout. Inx was killed by a trapper called Edgar Freemantle, who went on and only wounded that 'breed scout. He's still alive and kicking as far as I know.'

'Not what we heard,' said Billy excitedly. 'We read it all in the journals, how you made that daring escape from the prison. Killing those two guards and three prisoners as you went. Hell, set me all afire that did.'

'What!' gasped Johnny in surprise, then he did a double take. 'You fellows can read now?'

'And write. And do numbers, though I ain't so good at that. They teached us,' supplied Billy.

'You are one famous man,' said Adam proudly. He sipped on his liquor, pulled a wry grimace and threw it in the fireplace, where the flames leapt high at contact with the raw alcohol. 'It was an inspiration to us,' Adam concluded.

'But I never did those things,' Johnny said limply.

'We couldn't it take no more,' Billy said over him.

'That's right,' agreed Adam. 'I was stuck with that ugly Widow Jenkins who wouldn't leave me alone, always fumbling with me and such. She only wanted to make a husband out of me and Billy here was one of a troup of German brats whose ma couldn't stop giving orders and adding to the litter like a sow hog with piglets.'

'Didn't like it,' said Billy dolefully. 'Didn't like it at all.'

'So we got together and decided to light out, just like you did.' Adam smiled proudly.

'But you're road agents.'

'Sure are, Johnny Cable,' said Billy proudly. 'We got our own gang too. There's six of us now, call ourselves the Hellblazing Gang. What d'you think of that?'

Johnny was stunned by their proud admissions. In his life of studied avoidance and with no ability to read he had no idea that such falsehoods had spread about him. He had acquired a notoriety he never even knew about and his brothers had taken it all on board as an example of how to be.

'Look here, Johnny,' said Adam. 'There's nigh on a hundred and twenty-five thousand dollars in gold in that box out there; least, that's what we reckon. Come along of us, we'll cut you in. Think on it, the three Cable brothers. Robbing and killing. Why, we'll make such a name.'

'Yeah,' breathed Billy with obvious pleasure.

'I don't think so, boys. Look here, there's things you should know — '

Johnny was interrupted by a loud yell from outside.

'They got it!' cried Billy, rushing for the door.

'Come on, come look at the gold,' said Adam, following him out.

Johnny followed them to the doorway and watched the excited silhouettes in the darkness of the coach interior. He saw the rushing spill of sparkling gold coins flowing like a river through grasping fingers in the light from the doorway.

How could it have come to this? he wondered. Not only his own name a byword for misdeeds but now his brothers riding on the coat tails of that misunderstanding. He stood there, leaning against the doorpost wondering what he should do about it as the gang laughed joyously, filling their saddle-bags to overflowing.

When they were done Adam came over, a bulging pair of saddle-bags slung heavily over his forearm.

'You coming, brother?' he asked. 'We

got to get on now. You're welcome, you know that. Be pleased to have you with us.'

Johnny shook his head. 'No, Adam. You boys ride on, I'm going to stay with the stage.'

Adam grinned, his teeth white in the shadows. 'I know what you're about. Billy told me about that pretty young thing in there. You got your cap set, ain't you?'

Johnny lowered his eyes and shook his head ambiguously.

'Well, luck to you, Johnny. You keep riding that stage and doubtless we'll meet up again.' Adam chuckled.

Johnny looked up sharply. 'Don't you do that, Adam. I don't want to look down the barrel of a gun at my own brother.'

Adam shrugged, 'OK then, we'll leave the Leggett & Fox line alone, that's a promise. Railroad has more to offer now anyway.'

'Get out of this, Adam,' Johnny begged. 'It'll go badly for you both.'

'Ach,' snorted Adam. 'Not on your life. Things are too good for us. Look at this.' He raised the saddle-bag flap to show the glinting pile of coins inside. 'Just think on it; if Ma and Pa were alive, what we could do for them now.'

'But they ain't alive, are they? Just make sure you and Billy Boy don't go joining them sooner than you think.'

'We're going to live for ever,' Adam promised with a laugh. He turned away and disappeared into the shadows. 'I'll leave your passengers their possibles as a goodwill gesture. Make sure you let them know it was Adam Cable and the Hellblazers who done it,' he called over his shoulder.

'See you, Johnny!' Billy's cheerful call came out of the night followed by the sound of horses pounding off into the darkness. Dust rose up slowly over the roof of the Titan coach and, hanging in the air, formed a brown cloud across the moon. Johnny watched it for a moment before walking sadly over to the locked barn doors.

13

Later, as the moon rose higher in the night sky, a subdued set of passengers continued their journey onward through the night. The Titan driver had already left, determined to find succour for his wounded guard, carry the dead man and report the theft to the nearest authorities. Johnny waved a goodbye to Acer Smith as with a whoop and a holler Gunny whipped up the team and the Concord swayed on its leather springs, leaned into the curve away from the station and bumped back on to the worn ruts of the Southern Cheyenne Trail.

Even Gunny was quiet now, forgoing his usual raucous rendering and satisfying himself with only a few curses and whistles over the heads of the racing team. Normally, Johnny enjoyed this part of the journey sitting high up on the driving-box, the thundering hoofs pounding away below as they ate up the miles. The night air was fresh after the hot day and he felt a comfortable satisfaction as the swaying coach lurched over the bumpy pot-holed trail in Gunny's firm hands.

But this was not a night like any other. Johnny still fretted over the tales his brothers had told him and he shrank again into the sense of isolation he had experienced during his earlier years after his escape from prison. There seemed to be no release from acts that were none of his doing; whatever he did seemed always to turn out wrong. Was he born unlucky? he wondered. At fault from the beginning? Had Edgar Freemantle been right in his superstitious beliefs? Was there some curse that hung over his head, an unlucky star he had been born under?

'You knew them boys back there, huh?' Gunny's question broke into his ponderings.

Johnny nodded, 'Yep, I did.'

'None of my affair, you realize. Don't mean to pry an' all. Tell me to shut it if you've a mind but we've travelled a while so I'll reckon you'll let her slide.'

'It's OK,' said Johnny. 'I don't mind, Gunny. They was my brothers, the damn fools. Haven't seen them in years and now they pop up here riding the outlaw trail.' Johnny shook his head in dismay.

'Hey,' said Gunny understandingly. 'We all cut up some when we're young. I dursn't tell you the things I got up to in my day. They'll get past it.'

'I sure hope so,' said Johnny doubtfully.

'How'd you get separated?'

'Our folks died and the townsfolk took each of us in. I ended up with the real devil of a family and lit out early when it all turned sour.'

'You been running ever since, I guess.'

'That's the truth of it, Gunny. Can't say my life has been one big success so far.'

Gunny took time to slap the reins on his left-hand leader and drag on the one on the right, who was pulling too hard. 'Well, there's time, boy. It ain't over yet.'

Johnny leant forward on his knees as they hit a level patch of hard-packed sand on the trail. 'Beats me though, Gunny. Those boys, they thought I was some kind of hotshot roughneck and wanted nothing more than to copy my ways. Hell, I ain't no roughneck but every way I turn it ends up like I'm walking in horse manure. I tell you the truth, Gunny, I got crimes pasted on me that I swear I never committed and those two brothers, they think it's all ice cream on apple pie.'

'Everybody got to choose his own way, Johnny.'

'It's my fault, Gunny. Maybe it's all wrong, but they think they should be like me.'

'That's their choice, boy. 'Taint your fault if a body decides to follow the outlaw way, whatever their damned reasons.'

Johnny shook his head. 'I feel responsible, is all.'

'I know you don't see it from your end but when you get to my age you'll see that life's too short to go sweating on other folks and their ways. Just you make sure to get it right and let them go to hell in their own handcart.'

With that final piece of advice Gunny cracked the long whip over the horses' heads and called a loud halloo. 'Get along, dang you!' he bawled. 'We got a schedule to keep and we're running behind.'

But his advice was of little help to Johnny; he understood where Gunny came from. The old man was a lone wolf and had lived with that insular perspective probably for all of his life. He knew little of family or the bond that endured from childhood and despite the intervening years Johnny still remembered the golden days when he and Adam and Billy Boy had grown up freely, surrounded by a hard-working but loving family. The ties that bound him were woven into the fabric of his nature and he could not rid himself of the sense of responsibility he still felt for his brothers.

14

A day later they were heading into their driver changeover at Julesville, with only Joanna Moore leaving the coach. There had been little time for Johnny to converse further with the young school-teacher but he had enjoyed the moments they were able to spend together at the swing stations whilst the horses were changed and was sorry that the two of them would be parting ways soon.

The frontier town of Julesville that they rode into had begun life as a trading post built by an irascible Frenchman Jules Benoit who, it was said, had killed many men and taken their ears as souvenirs, which he would keep in his pocket to display to the impressionable. It had been a busy crossroads point for both Sioux and Cheyenne in earlier times and the

Indians had frequented and traded at the popular post, thus ensuring its growth in later years.

The town was built on two levels of flat land, the original log cabins and tent canvas supplemented structures still existed on the lower level, which Johnny had advised Joanna to avoid. Here congregated a rough and ready populace who strip-mined for coal in the nearby workings or toiled in the various attached industries that had grown up. In all it was a growing town, bursting with sudden wealth and all that attends to it. Whorehouses and drinking palaces abounded, where gambling and general mayhem were commonplace and the regular toll of violent deaths filled the cemetery that marked the entrance to the town.

Right now, the streets of the lower town were a quagmire as a recent heavy storm had run down and left pools of churned mud that could be crossed only by the use of long planks. The stink it made was beginning to rise up the slope to the wealthier upper town as over-flooded outhouses added their ripe odour to the already reeking swamp of undrained soil. Bugs proliferated with the coming warmth and the already foul air was filled with swarms of blowflies and mosquitoes.

The upper town, though, was high enough to benefit to some degree from a breeze that kept the air clear. The families of more genteel merchants and mine-owners, who looked down on their lower neighbours with a self-righteous forbearance had settled there. They needed workers for their mines and factories, so the two categories stayed at close quarters if a little ill at ease. The desire of these wealthier patrons for self-improvement had provided the incentive to advertise in Eastern newspapers for a suitable educator for their children. It was in such a way that Joanna had been selected to administer their new-built schoolhouse and brought out West with the promise of a good wage and her own accommodation.

A town marshal called Jack Slade policed the city limits at the behest of the wealthy, but it was debatable whether he was much better than the roughnecks he dealt with. His methods were questionable and certainly outside the letter of the law but as most successful lawmen of the day he achieved results and the wealthy townspeople chose to ignore his brutal pistol whippings and bloody shootouts for the sake of a quiet life.

Jack Slade was a tall, solidly built man with stern features and a neatly clipped moustache; he favoured a garishly decorated silk waistcoat, frock-coat and flat-topped Stetson. His cross-draw pistol was always kept on prominent display below the silver shield of office he kept tacked to the waistcoat under his jacket. He was standing on the boardwalk next to the change-over driver and shotgun guard who were ready to take the coach on through the next stage of its journey. He was fiddling self-consciously with his stickpin necktie when the Concord eventually turned in and pulled up before the Legget & Fox Stage Line offices.

'How do, Gunny,' he called up as Gunny tugged on the brake lever. 'How'd it go this trip? Any trouble I should hear about?'

'Only the Titan getting robbed. You must've heard about that?' Gunny answered, as Johnny jumped down and started to undo the baggage flap at the rear of the coach.

'Yep, it passed through earlier. Left a man with the doctor and one with the undertaker. It was the Cable boys and the Hellblazing Gang, so the driver said. They give you any trouble?'

'Nope,' said Gunny avoiding his eyes whilst Johnny buried himself furtively amongst the luggage. 'Nary a thing.'

'You were lucky,' said the marshal. 'How come they passed you by?'

'Guess they had their fill with the bullion. We were small pickings after that haul.'

'True enough. You see 'em at work?'

Gunny flapped his glove at the dust coating his buffalo skin and raised a white cloud. 'Yes sir, we were up at the Forty Rod station when they took the Titan. Killed one and wounded another, then got clean away.'

'And they just left you be?'

Gunny nodded without further reply as Johnny went round the far side of the coach and opened the door for Joanna.

'We're here, Miss Joanna,' he said. 'Let me help you down.'

'Thank you, Johnny.' She took his hand as he gave her room to dismount. 'So this is Julesville.' She looked around curiously.

'This is it, ma'am. Step careful though. It's wet and slippery underfoot.'

Marshal Slade bustled around the side of the coach. 'Why, what have we here?' he said cheerfully. 'The new schoolmarm, I'll be bound.' He touched his hat brim. 'Marshal Slade, at your service, ma'am.'

'Joanna Moore,' said Joanna with a slight curtsy. 'Pleased to meet you, Marshal.'

'Pleasure is mine. I've been sent along to escort you up to the schoolhouse. We can drop off your belongings and I'll take you to meet the town councillors. They'll be right pleased to see you.'

'Why, thank you, Marshal, I'd be most grateful.'

Johnny felt a twinge of jealousy at the intrusion of the marshal's attentions, although he did not quite understand why.

The marshal turned to him. 'You bring the lady's trunks up to the schoolhouse, fella,' he ordered curtly.

Johnny lowered his head below his hat brim in silence and nodded, not wanting to bring attention to himself. 'Sure enough,' he mumbled.

'Do you mind, Johnny?' asked Joanna, stepping forward and resting a hand on his arm. 'I'm sure I can hire a porter if you're busy with the coach.'

'No trouble, miss,' Johnny answered quietly, already feeling the marshal's eyes on him at her use of his first name.

'Do I know you?' asked Slade suddenly.

Johnny met his gaze at last, 'I been up there riding shotgun beside Gunny for the past twelve month.'

'Funny,' said Slade. 'Can't say I've noticed you before.'

'Oh,' said Joanna brightly. 'Johnny's been most helpful and good company on a long and tiresome journey.'

'I'll bet he has,' said Slade doubtfully as Johnny bent to pick up the luggage. 'Well,' he shrugged, 'let's be getting along. Sounds like you've had an eventful trip all right, Miss Moore?'

Johnny, laden with luggage, glanced across at Gunny as he followed behind the marshal and the schoolteacher as they set off on the mud-slicked climb to the upper town. Gunny gave him an extravagant wink and chuckled wheezily into his grizzled beard.

* * *

When Johnny got back to the office Gunny was still giving him a knowing eye, but Johnny was having none of it. He was irritated and grumpy after watching the marshal and Joanna chatting away together as if he did not exist. He had dumped the luggage on the newly sawn wooden floor of the schoolhouse and hurried away.

'What's the matter?' asked Gunny, with a grin. 'You look like a rabid dog just licked your candy bar.'

'Leave off, Gunny. I ain't in the mood,' growled Johnny.

'You see that,' Gunny teased, turning to Ed Post, the station superintendent. 'Marshal Slade stepped into the picture 'tween Johnny and that sweet thing we just brought in on the stage and it's all discombobulated him.'

Ed Post, a slender, worried-looking man, with expanding metal garters on his shirtsleeves, a celluloid collar and green eyeshade, looked up from his paperwork and shook his head.

'Well, could be you'll get a second

chance, Johnny. Look here, you two, I've got some bad news for you both. The rain hit the eastbound stage with a mudslide. She went over the edge at Twin Rock on her way here. Hell of a mess. Leaves me in an awkward position, I can tell you. Going to have to let you fellers go unless you want to hang around until the westbound turns around and gets in again.'

'Hey, that's a bit sudden, Ed,' said Gunny with a frown.

'I know it,' said Ed. 'But look, Gunny, you've seen how it is. The railroads pressing in, we don't make enough to run more than two stages. It costs too much to keep all them swing stations going with blacksmiths, farriers and the like. It's a plain fact, our days are numbered here, the company bosses back East are about ready to cut their losses and close her down. You boys would be better off getting some other form of employment.'

Gunny scratched his unshaven chin dourly with a rasping sound. 'Some kind of turn-up this is, Ed. That's taken the wind out of my sails, I can tell you. I reckon I worked for this line for nigh on ten years. And now you're putting me out without a prayer in my pocket.'

'Well,' Ed shrugged, 'what can I tell you? I didn't lay the railway and it isn't my say so, I just work here, same as you. I already got me a clerking job lined up at Fort Havering, so you won't be seeing me much longer. Now, you want to take your wages and quit or hang on a while and wait for the eastbound? Can't pay you if you wait on it though, sorry about that.'

Gunny looked across at Johnny with a questioning look.

'How about we take our due and think on the rest, Ed?' said Johnny.

'Sure thing,' said Ed. 'Drop by tomorrow and I'll have your wages. I'll be here anyway, until that eastbound gets in. Reckon it'll be the last stage out of here.'

Johnny looked down sombrely at his mud-caked boots and began scraping them off on the edge of the door sill.

'Don't be doing that,' cried an irritated Ed Post. 'Come on, Johnny. What few customers we do get, come in here through that door. They don't want to be stepping over your pile of leavings. Now get on out of here and let me finish my bookwork, will you?'

'Aw, hell!' snarled Johnny irritably, plunging his hands into his pockets and hunching his back.

Gunny slapped him on the shoulder and laughed cheerfully. 'Come on, boy. Let's go eat, maybe get us a drink or two before we bed down. What d'you say? Something'll turn up and if that young miss is getting under your skin, you know no schoolteacher ain't going to look twice at a poor fellow like you. Or me, come to that, even when I was younger and more up to chasing pretty gels just for the fun of it.'

Disconsolately, Johnny followed the old man out on to the busy street. Gunny continued to chat away in an attempt to cheer Johnny up. Eventually his determination won through and Johnny laid aside his depression.

'Say, look,' said Gunny after they had eaten. 'Ed told me about this place in the lower town. Says it's something to see, got some kind of brand-new trade simulator machine fresh in from San Francisco. You want to try it?'

'Why not,' said Johnny. 'I could do with some diversion.'

'That's the spirit, son.'

Gunny led the way cautiously down the sharply angled slippery slope that led to the mire-covered lower town which was already crowded and resounding with the sounds of early-evening revelry. Music and raucous laughter filled the fetid air and drunken men staggered across the plank walkways, often in their stupor falling into the streaming mud below.

The dank alleyways and littered streets were filled with eating and gaming houses, saloons and whore-houses. Crude signs swung from a clutter of buildings fabricated from all kinds of materials, ranging from tin sheet to canvas. Drifting amongst them was the smell of roasting chickens mixed with the numbing stench of open drains.

Their destination occupied a prime position on the main street, a high, false-fronted wooden building with fresh paint and an extravagant sign above it. If Johnny could have read the sign he might well have had second thoughts about entering. Standing over the place in big bright letters embellished with glittering gold paint and under lit by oil lamps were the words 'Lash Lassiter's Eureka Loophole'. Below that hung lurid signs advertising the usual entertainment available in such establishments: poker, faro, keno, stud and Spanish monte. Plus the newest introduction from the coast: the Bell Machine.

They pushed their way into the crowded interior and passed the more serious players who sat, silently intent, at green-baize card tables. Dice and Spinning Wheel chancers pressed shoulder to shoulder with drinkers at the long, waist-high bartop, behind which sweating bartenders were rushed off their feet by the demand.

Feathered narrow-eyed cot girls, displaying their wares all too obviously, swam through the crowd looking for rich prey like hungry sharks in a fish pool. At one end on a small stage a pianist struggled to make himself heard above the din, but he was fighting a losing battle, his jangle only adding to the general din. On the walls hung dozens of tiny cages with chirping canaries fluttering inside, an indication of the mining men's need for early warning of the dangerous scentless gasses found at the mines.

Above the throng and all the deafening noise, the air inside the large, high-ceilinged room was thick with tobacco smoke and the stink of stale liquor that hung undisturbed like a miasma drifting above the heads of the customers.

Johnny and Gunny made their way to the bar and fought for a place in the queue that stood before the Bell Machine which was attracting so much attention. It stood at one end of the bar in a place of honour. A solid-looking, curlicue-decorated metal box of a machine, with a small slot window in front and a lever handle down one side.

Gunny tapped the fellow in front of them on the shoulder. 'What's the score on this here newfangled trade simulator?' he asked.

The fellow, a mining man still black with coal dust from his working day, turned and gave Gunny the once over before answering, 'You put your money in that there hole in the top, see?' Gunny nodded. 'Then you pull the lever down and them three wheels inside starts spinning. You got horseshoes, spades, diamonds, hearts and bells. You can get a flush, or two of a kind for a pay-out but the bells in a line wins you the big one.'

'That so? And what's that?'

'Well, it says ten free drinks on the front but that's just to get around the gambling laws. What it actually does is give you coin.'

'Money!' said Gunny. 'Hell! That's a new one. How much d'you get?'

'Three bells will bring you fifty cents.'

'Hot damn! Cash money instead of cigars and drinks.' Gunny grinned. 'I got to have me some of that.'

Johnny though, was losing interest; he could see it would be a long wait until Gunny got his chance to play. Already men in the queue were fighting over how many turns a body should have. He rested his elbows up on the bar behind him and casually looked around at the heaving crowd.

Suddenly the room seemed to lose focus for a moment, the restless crowd blurring as his attention zeroed in on one man. Saloon customers appeared to part like the Red Sea as the man made his way in an almost regal fashion towards the bar. Johnny felt his insides cringe as he recognized the character brushing his way towards him. Little had changed in the intervening years. Still fat and burly, though his unshaven double chin now sported a drooping moustache hanging over it from the upper lip. Boss Lassiter looked just as mean and greasy as he had back at Gomar penitentiary.

He was dressed differently, sporting a chequered necktie and striped waistcoat under a clean, cream-coloured and neatly pressed drape jacket and pants. His one item of dress that clashed was the leather gunbelt carrying the gleaming rolled bullwhip that he still favoured. He came without faltering and Johnny dropped his hands to his sides in anticipation. They were inches apart when Lassiter brushed in beside Johnny and leant forward, rapping a fist on the bartop and bringing the head bartender hastily over.

'Yeah, Lash. Help you?'

'How are we doing here tonight?' Lassiter asked, hoisting a thumb in the direction of the Bell Machine.

He was so close that Johnny could smell the pomade on Lassiter's hair and the wash of eau de cologne that he doused himself with. Johnny stared steadfastly ahead, holding himself taut, his muscles bunched in anticipation of the moment Lassiter would recognize him. He did not dare to move, and froze rigidly, keeping his gaze fixed firmly ahead.

'Couldn't be better,' said the bar-tender. 'Suckers can't get enough of it. I've had to empty the cash bucket twice already.'

Lassiter wheezed a laugh. 'Good. Cost me a pretty-enough penny. Looks like she might pay for herself soon, though.'

'Hell,' said the bartender. 'We make enough over the bar every night to pay for ten more of the things.'

Lassiter half-smiled and arched a speculative eyebrow. 'That's not a bad idea. Not bad at all. Give me a bourbon, will you?'

'Sure, boss.'

'I told you already,' snapped Lassiter, suddenly angry, 'never to call me that. It's Lash or Mr Lassiter. Never 'boss'. You got it?'

'Sorry b — er, Lash. I . . . um . . . forgot. I'll get your bourbon.'

Lassiter breathed deeply and turned to look over the crowded heads of his saloon. Johnny promptly moved around so that his back was to Lassiter. He elbowed Gunny in the side.

'I guess I'll turn in, Gunny,' he said. 'I'm not much fun tonight.'

Gunny was full of anticipation, his attention firmly fixed on the head of the queue. 'I'll be along directly,' he said vaguely. 'Just got to have me a go or two on this thing here. Damn! Ain't modern science wonderful? Imagine, a machine that pays out money.'

Not much of it, thought Johnny, *not if Boss Lassiter is behind it.*

Johnny raised his hand to straighten

the brim of his hat and hide his face, then passed Lassiter and vanished into the crowd, heading for the door and the sanctuary of the night.

15

The appearance of his old prison guard caused Johnny to fret over the next few days. He had no liking to be in the near vicinity of either Boss Lassiter or his own errant brothers. One or other of them could easily bring trouble into his life again. Gunny meanwhile, it appeared, was fixated by the Bell Machine to an almost manic degree and spent long hours losing every cent he possessed pumping the addictive machine to little avail. Johnny was left very much to his own devices during these days of waiting.

The weather had brightened and the storm clouds disappeared, leaving a hot sun to bake the muddy streets dry. Under the tramping of many feet the churned surface was soon turned again to beaten dust. During these days Johnny felt an all-pervasive desire to see the schoolteacher again. Joanna had been in his thoughts ever since they had received news of the stageline's closure and he found himself almost unconsciously drawn up towards the schoolhouse.

She was unpacking books from a crate when he arrived. The single, large room still smelt strongly of fresh-cut pine and the windows had not yet acquired a coating of grime, so it was bright inside with the sunlight streaming in. At one end a large blackboard had been fixed to the wall and rows of little desks were laid out before it. Vases of wild flowers stood on the window-sills, pasqueflower, larkspur, blue flag and Indian paintbrush brought splashes of vibrant colour to the room.

Johnny removed his hat and stood at the door, waiting for her to notice him. 'Howdy, ma'am,' he said after a few moments.

She looked up, shading her eyes and unable to distinguish more than a black silhouette with the sunlight behind. 'Yes?' she said. 'Who is it?'

'Me, ma'am. Johnny Dollar.'

'Johnny!' She smiled. 'How nice to see you. Come on in, please do.'

Coyly, he approached down the aisle between the desks. 'Looks real fine in here, Miss Joanna.'

She nodded happily. 'Yes, I'm very pleased with it. Imagine, my very own schoolhouse. But how are things with you, Johnny?'

'Not so good, I'm afraid. We got laid off. It appears they're closing the stageline down.'

'That's too bad.' She frowned. 'What will you do now?'

Johnny shrugged. 'Don't know as yet. We'll find something, I guess. What're you doing there?' he asked, indicating the crate.

'Just schoolbooks,' she said, handing him a primer.

Johnny took the booklet and opened it, looking at the large pictures inside. Johnny shook his head.

'Wish I knew the meaning,' he said, thumbing the pages.

'You never learnt?' asked Joanna.

'No, ma'am. My folks had no learning and there wasn't a school like this around where I grew up.'

She looked at him thoughtfully, a gentle smile playing on her lips. 'Look here, it's easy. I'll show you.' She opened the book and pointed at a picture of an apple. 'You know what that is, don't you?'

'Sure,' he said.

'Well you see that letter next to it?'

'That thing like a mountain with a bar across the middle?'

'That's the letter 'A'. And 'A' is for apple.'

'Uhuh,' said Johnny. 'It kind of looks like a brand on a cow.'

'Yes, it does, doesn't it? And that's how it works, Johnny. Each bunch of letters strung together has a meaning, it signifies what that particular cow is. But, look here . . . ' she swiftly turned pages. 'See this one? What do you make out there?'

'Looks to me like a mousey kind of creature.'

'It is, it's a mouse . . . and the letter next to it?'

'That two mountains joined together thing?'

'The letter 'M' . . . 'M' is for mouse,' she stressed the first letter, almost humming it.

'So 'M' is the brand on a mouse?'

'Well, only the beginning letter. Look I'll show you.'

She crossed to the blackboard, took up a piece of chalk and wrote out the letters M-O-U-S-E in capitals.

'There,' she said. 'The whole group of letters together is the brand for a mouse. It's the brand that belongs only to that creature.'

Johnny nodded dubiously. 'Sure, I see,' he said vaguely.

Joanna looked long at Johnny. She liked him and felt comfortable in his presence; she knew he was a simple man and was sure he had suffered hard beginnings, but still she felt he was a honourable sort of fellow and that all his experiences throughout his tough life had not undermined his natural upright character. In all, she saw a fine young man before her and her own natural inclinations as a teacher rose within her.

'Would you like to learn, Johnny?'

'Learn to read?'

She nodded.

Johnny smiled with doubtful awkwardness. 'Don't know as I fit into one of these here benches. Kind of long in the leg — and the tooth for that matter.'

Joanna shook her head. 'It's never too late to learn, Johnny. I can give you some lessons outside of school time, if you like. It would mean coming here after the children have left for the day, but I'm sure you'd be reading in no time at all. What do you say? It would be my pleasure.'

Johnny liked the sound of that. In reality he felt no need for reading or writing; he had managed for years without the skills but the prospect of being near to this pretty girl and having her personal attention was an offer he could not refuse.

'I reckon I would like that, Miss Joanna. It's kind of you.'

'Well,' she shrugged with a happy grin, 'it's decided then. You have the time on your hands now and we must make the most of it. I warn you though, Johnny, I will work you hard.'

'I ain't afraid of that, ma'am.'

'But this is different work. It's headwork. Not the muscles in your arm, which I'm sure are mighty strong, but the ones in your head, which probably need the exercise.'

'I'll do my best, Miss Joanna.'

16

It became interesting for Johnny over the next few weeks to see Joanna in a new light. In the schoolroom she was not the excited and impressionable young woman he had first met on the stage; here she was a brisk and businesslike personality, forthright with her praise and her criticism alike. She took his education in hand with an easy fervour and under her tuition he proved a capable student, mastering the alphabet readily. Joanna in her turn was surprised with the agility of Johnny's brain and pleased to see the alacrity with which he handled his studies.

He sat cramped in one of the small desks, his long legs spread wide into the alleyway. He had a slate before him upon which he copied the letter combinations that she set out on the blackboard. Johnny could not but want her attentions and he would frequently ask questions just to have her come and stand over him, her curling hair brushing his cheek as she made corrections. The smell of her perfume lingered in his mind long after their lessons were over and the memory of the warmth of her small hand over his as she guided his writing fingers was a touch he was hard put to forget.

Johnny knew his heart was going out to the woman but any declarations of such a nature froze in his embarrassed throat. He felt that, as Gunny had observed, it was most unlikely that any educated creature as fine as she could ever entertain the notion of an alliance with an illiterate man like himself. But still he nursed his affections secretly and the flame was fanned brighter in his breast by their regular daily contact.

They were occupied in their studies late one afternoon, when they were interrupted by the appearance of Marshal Slade.

'Why,' he said, coming in noisily, his

boots thumping on the bare floor-boards. 'A special lesson in progress. I had no idea you took on adult students, Miss Joanna.'

Joanna turned to look at him with a ready smile. 'How are your reading and writing skills, Marshal?' she asked.

'Not to worry, missy. I have my letters well and good already.' He looked down at Johnny and raised one curious eyebrow. 'We've met before, I think.'

'Yes sir,' said Johnny. 'I rode shotgun at the stageline.'

'That's right, I remember now.' Slade paused, looking up at Joanna and paying no further attention to Johnny as he continued: 'Reason I'm here, Joanna, is that they have a soirée up at the church tonight. Some piano pieces and choral too, I think. I thought perhaps you might accompany me, if you've a mind?'

'Why that sounds most pleasant, Marshal. I had no idea you held such an inclination for music,'

He chuckled. 'In all truth, ma'am, I

have no sense of melody at all. I just thought it would be something you might prefer as there is little else of genteel entertainment in this town.'

'I'd be most happy to attend,' she said. 'Thank you for the invite.'

Johnny felt the marshal standing beside him puff up with contentment, as a man might who was sure of the outcome already but doubly pleased when it came to fruition as he had imagined it. Johnny's head was level with the man's waist and his sidelong glance caught the yellowish shine of the bonehandled pistol strapped crosswise in the marshal's gunbelt. It looked a well-used piece, the leather of the holster smooth and black with oil. Johnny thought he caught a whiff of the weapon. It smelt of cold steel, lead and of death.

'Very well,' said Slade. 'I shall call on — '

'Marshal!' The call came from the doorway. A boy was standing there, panting hard.

'What is it?' asked Slade.

'You'd better come. Mr Lassiter sent me, he has trouble down at his place.'

'What sort of trouble?' asked Slade quickly, his eyes keen and businesslike now.

'Some cow men come in drunk and they're looking to get into a fight with the miners.'

'How many of them?'

'A parcel of trail herders. About ten miners or so, I ain't sure 'xactly.'

'A good-sized bust-up then.' Slade frowned. 'All right, I'll be there.' He paused, about to go to the door. 'You, fella,' he said, pointing at Johnny. 'You rode shotgun, you can do the same for me. You're deputized. Come along.' He glanced briefly at Joanna, 'Miss Joanna, excuse me, duty calls.'

Johnny sat still with a sinking feeling in his stomach, looking up from one to the other of them.

'Come on, boy. Shake a leg,' ordered Slade briskly. 'We'll pick up a shotgun and shells at the stageline office on the way down.'

Johnny could see no alternative. Slowly he got to his feet and with bitterly compressed lips and an apologetic shrug at Joanna he followed the marshal out.

They went at a fast pace, stopping only to collect the shotgun and ammunition from Ed Post at the office.

'You back me up, understand?' Slade said as he strode down the hillside. 'Leave the talking to me and keep out of my line of fire.'

Johnny nodded as he cracked open the double barrel and slid two shells in.

'What's your name again, I forgot?' asked Slade.

'Johnny,' he answered evasively.

'OK, Johnny. Stay alert and see that none of these sidewinders comes up on my back.'

Their boots clattered on the boardwalk as they ran up the steps and into Lash Lassiter's Eureka Loophole.

A regular brawl was in progress.

Cowhands, obvious in their dust-stained chaps and colourful wool shirts were in a fiery set-to with muddy miners dressed in shabby clothing. Fists flew and furniture splintered, broken glass was scattered on the sawdust covered floor and back against the walls stood an array of watching customers, cheering and revelling at the free entertainment.

The pianist on his small stage continued to play a brisk polka. He kept looking nervously over his shoulder as he played, occasionally ducking as a thrown missile appeared from the fighting crowd and smashed against the wall behind him.

Slade did not hesitate. With barely a glance at the sparring men he waded in, pistol drawn. His gun hand flew this way and that, the pistol barrel bouncing off heads without favour. The gun butt downed two men who stood in his path without a moment's hesitation as his burly body forced its way towards the bar. Johnny followed the path the marshal cleaved through the fighting men, ducking and weaving, the shotgun held high as fists and bottles were thrown his way.

A grimacing cowhand stood before him, eyes wide and a slick of blood colouring his teeth where his lip had been split. With clawing hands the man reached out to grab at Johnny, who quickly swung up the shotgun butt, catching the fellow a crack under the jaw. The cowhand dropped away and Johnny continued onwards, trying to catch up with the marshal who had forged ahead and was almost at the bar. Slade turned and loosed off a shot ceiling wards. A cloud of splinters fell about him as he bellowed, 'That's enough, boys. I'm Marshal Slade and I'll down any man who argues.'

At sound of the gunshot the mayhem abated somewhat, and only a few who were too immersed in the struggle continued. But they too soon saw the fight was over and stood, arms hanging, their chests heaving, with bloody grins on their bruised faces.

'Hell of a fight, Marshal,' came a call. 'Why'd you have to stop her?'

'Cos I'm the law here, is why,' shouted Slade in response.

Lassiter made an appearance then, coming out from a crowded corner. 'Obliged, Marshal,' he growled. 'But who's going to pay for all this?' He waved a hand over the debris littering the floor.

'Who started it?' asked Slade, his pistol still held ready.

Johnny moved away along one side of the bar, cocking both barrels of the shotgun as he did so.

'Come on,' insisted Slade. 'Let's have it. Which of you was it?'

A slanging match began with miners accusing cowboys and the cowboys blaming the miners. Slade let them continue their shouting for a few minutes before calling for order again.

'This is how it plays out, boys,' he said. 'Seeing as you can't agree, both parties shell out for the damages in equal amounts. Now, you've all had your fun, so see Lash here gets his money for the things you've busted.'

Johnny noticed Gunny then, standing stooped amongst the watching crowd. He gave him a nod of recognition but was disappointed when the old-timer barely looked back at him. He appeared to be in a poor way and Johnny was determined to find out the cause later.

The miners and cowboys began smiling now that an accord had been reached. Slapping each other on the back and laughing, they headed for the bar for friendly drinks all round. Slade holstered his pistol and Johnny was lowering the shotgun when he saw a shape moving fast through the crowd. A knife blade flashed in the dim light and the shape took on the lean body of a cowhand, teeth gleaming and eyes intent on the marshal's unprotected back.

Slade took the blade high in the right shoulder, the thump forcing him to stagger forward with a cry. His attacker howled and pulled out the blade, a broad-bladed Bowie knife, and he swung it back ready to strike again. 'To the devil with you, lawman!' he screamed.

Johnny shouted for the men around him to duck, then he let loose with both barrels. It was as if the cowhand had been caught suddenly by a fierce wind. He flew across the room, taking both barrels of shot side on, limbs whirled as he crashed against the watching crowd, some of whom caught some of the spreading buckshot as well. The fellow flopped down in a rubbery tumble of torn clothing, the Bowie knife spinning from his hand. Clutching his wounded shoulder, Slade turned angrily, pistol in hand; without pause he fired three shots into the downed cowhand.

'Damn!' he spat, looking at his blood stained fingers. 'Rat-tailed backstabber. Look what he's done to my best Sunday jacket.' His eyes glanced up from the wound and nodded at Johnny. 'Saved my neck from worse, I guess.

You got my thanks, Johnny.'

Johnny kept his head down, as he split the shotgun and ejected the spent shell casings before reloading. Already though, he had noticed with a twist of apprehension that Lassiter's eyes had fallen on him with a curious glint.

17

Johnny had hoped that the marshal's wound would keep him from escorting Joanna that evening, but he was to be disappointed in that. The marshal, his arm in a sling, showed himself at Joanna's door on time and Johnny watched in dismay as Slade strode off with Joanna on his good arm. He heard her sympathetic noises and Slade's bold denial of any inconvenience, saying the wound was nothing but a scratch and not to be bothered with.

There is nothing so despairing as unrequited love in a young man, and despite all his boldness Johnny felt only a hollow emptiness inside, blaming himself for his caution and lack of willingness to declare himself openly to Joanna. The advent of Slade on the scene did nothing to ease his aching heart. The forceful and capable figure of the marshal was an undeniably strong contender for Joanna's favour, and daily he imagined her slipping away from him and into Slade's powerful arms. The added regret for him was the fact that Joanna appeared to welcome the lawman's attentions.

He made his way back down to the lower town in search of Gunny, to find out how the old-timer was doing. He did not really want to enter the Eureka Loophole again, but he felt his friend was a higher call than his nervousness about Lassiter.

The place was its usual self, bursting at the seams and as noisy as it might be. Johnny favoured the wall side of the room, threading his way through the crowd and trying to be as inconspicuous as possible. His eyes searched the bustling customers, looking for Gunny. Although the press was heaviest around the Bell Machine there was no sign of Gunny in that direction. Then he saw the old man; he was down on his knees, a bucket and broom beside him, scrabbling amongst the sawdust beside a table of card players. Johnny made his way over to him through the press.

'What are you doing down there, Gunny?' he asked when he stood over the kneeling figure.

Gunny looked up and Johnny saw the tired lines on his yellowish skin, the hollowness of his eyes and the bruised bags beneath. Gunny winced as he recognized Johnny and bit his lip.

'There's dust here,' he said, clutching a handful of sawdust.

'Dust?' asked Johnny. 'What d'you mean?'

Gunny got up and pulled at Johnny's sleeve, tugging him out of earshot away from the card playing tables.

'Them prospectors,' he confided. 'They spill it from their pokes when they're playing. See, I wash it out and gets a piece every time.' He opened his clenched fist and amongst the sawdust Johnny could just make out a few pitifully small shining flakes, which he took to be gold.

'Are you that broke?' Johnny asked, trying to hide the disgust from his face as he smelt the old man's unwashed clothes and body tainted with the ripe reek of whiskey.

Gunny shrugged. 'I guess I went a bit too far on that there Bell Machine. That and a bottle or two.'

'You mean you've lost all your quitting pay on that fool machine and then you started drinking. What the hell's the matter with you?'

Gunny shrugged and answered a little angrily. 'What else am I to do? No one'll hire me, they all say I'm too old now. They want the youngsters for haulage. Mr Lassiter here, he gives me something for clearing up glasses and sweeping out.'

Johnny frowned at that. 'What about the lumber and coal yard? They'll need a teamster I'll be bound.'

'Same story. This town is jumping, there's plenty of young blood about. Cheap and easy to hire; me, I'm just old news now.'

'Don't be so damned silly, Gunny. Why, you've more experience in your little finger than any of these boys.'

'Them that's hiring calls the tune, Johnny boy,' Gunny said sadly.

Johnny shook his head. 'When did you last eat?' he asked.

Gunny looked away vaguely to a corner of the bustling room. 'Can't say I rightly recall.'

'Come on,' urged Johnny. 'I'll stand you a meal. I've still got some cash left.'

'I'd rather have a shot, Johnny. Could you stand me that?'

'Not on your life, Gunny,' Johnny said firmly. 'Now you come along with me. We're getting out of here and get you cleaned up and fed.'

'I ain't got anywhere particular now,' Gunny complained plaintively. 'Ed threw me out of the bunkhouse. Said I smelt like a goat.'

'He was right. But we'll see about that once you've taken a trip to the bathhouse.'

The black-braided two-bellied leather

line cracked across Gunny's wrist and whirled about it with an unpleasant flashing sheen, like a long rattler striking.

'Where d'you think you're going, Gunny?'

It was Lassiter. He unflicked the end of the twelve-foot bullwhip and began rolling it in. 'There's work to do here. Get your idle backside around those tables and pick up the empties.'

Gunny cringed, sucking at his wrist where a red weal was already developing. 'Yessir, Mr Lassiter. Sorry about that.'

Although Johnny had stepped back away from Gunny at the appearance of Lassiter, he looked at his friend with sadness as the old man bowed obsequiously before the strutting saloon owner.

'Go on, get along,' Lassiter snarled coldly. 'Or I'll whup your sorry ass good.'

Johnny's anger rose then and, despite his earlier fears, it spilled over. He tensed as cold bitterness filled him. 'Who the devil are you to treat an old man like that?' he snapped, stepping forward.

A quietness descended on those near enough to hear what was going on and a small pool of silence began to spread in the general chaos surrounding them.

Lassiter shrugged, thinking Johnny was just another customer. 'He's only an old soak who cleans up around here. Don't pay him no heed.'

'No, I'm talking about you, Mr Lassiter. How come you whip him like a dog? Make you feel big, does it, beating on an old man like that?'

'Aw, come on, feller. It was no more than a tickle. Don't get all wound up about it. You know, I've got a busy place here, I have to keep the staff in line . . . '

Johnny swiftly crossed the gap between them, pushing his face close up to Lassiter's. 'Just you treat him right in future, you understand me?'

Lassiter pulled back, surprised, a questioning look in his eye, 'You're the deputy that came in with Slade today and shot that cowpoke, right?'

Johnny continued to stare hard into Lassiter's eyes. 'Better remember it,' he warned.

'Or what?' Lassiter sneered.

'Just maybe I'll come by and pop your cork too.'

Lassiter's gaze lowered now, his shoulders hunching as a calculating coldness entered into his eyes. He met Johnny's stare head on, his features frozen and his fat jaw set tight. 'You come try any time, boy.'

Johnny continued to stare at Lassiter as he backed away and took Gunny by the sleeve.

'Forget it, Mr Lassiter,' the old man whined. 'Johnny don't mean nothing by it. Really he don't.'

Johnny looked at him in surprise, he could not believe that Gunny, the bold stagecoach driver who had braved so many dangers, could sink so low as to bow down before this bullying oaf.

'What're you saying, Gunny?' he asked quietly.

Gunny pulled away from him. 'I got to stay here, Johnny. It's my meal ticket. I got to stay.'

'Don't do it, man,' said Johnny. 'I'll see you're all right. Come along with me.'

'No, no. You go on. I'll be OK.' Gunny looked pleadingly at Lassiter. 'It's all right, ain't it Mr Lassiter?'

Lassiter looked at them both, his confidence returning. 'Sure it is, Gunny. You go on over to the bar and get yourself a drink, tell them I said so.' His eyes never left Johnny as the old man scurried off, pushing his way hungrily through the crowd of watchers. 'I know you from somewhere, don't I? I've seen your face before, but I can't place you yet.'

'Funny that,' hissed Johnny coldly. 'I remember you well enough . . . Boss Lassiter.'

Lassiter's eyes rounded as he got the message, his mouth opened to make a reply but Johnny was gone, slipping back into the crowd and leaving quickly.

18

In a way Johnny was glad it was out in the open. He felt a wave of relief as the need for caution slipped away from him. It was as if a weight had been lifted. It became clear to him then that despite Lassiter's knowing about his prison time, the ex-guard captain probably had no desire for others to know of his own origins either. There were plenty of released prisoners about who would remember Lassiter's cruel treatment and perhaps they might like to pay him a revenge visit one dark night. Lassiter would not want that; he had too much to lose now.

As Johnny walked back to his lodgings he pondered on that fact. Just how had an ex-prison guard on a miserable state-paid wage managed to set himself up with a brand-new saloon, ready built and stocked. It would need a pretty penny to do that. Shipping in timber, paying a builder, setting up gaming tables, beer and liquor and staff. It would be something worth looking into. He lay awake and spent a long night considering that notion.

The next day when Johnny arrived and saw Joanna in the schoolhouse, he noticed a difference in her right away. She seemed nervy, her eyes looked red-rimmed and her brow drawn and troubled.

'Something wrong, Miss Joanna?' he asked as he eased himself awkwardly into a small desk and drew a slate towards himself, ready to start the lesson.

'I wonder, Johnny,' she said, taking a deep breath. 'Would you mind if we gave today a miss. I don't feel too well.'

'Of course not,' he said, getting up quickly. 'But tell me, what is it. Is there anything I can do?'

'No,' she said hurriedly with a flutter of her fingers. 'It's nothing really.'

Johnny could see her obvious distress

and moved to her. 'Tell me.'

'No . . . it's . . . no . . . ' She turned away but not before he had seen the trickle of a tear running from her eye. Quickly she wiped her cheek with the fingers of her hand. 'Forgive me,' she said.

'Joanna,' his voice was a whisper. He could not bear to see her like this and any earlier inhibition he might have had felt fell away instantly. 'Nothing will harm you, I'll see to that.'

At his words she turned quickly to him and fell gratefully into his arms, her face pressed deep into his shoulder. 'It was Jack,' she sobbed, her voice muffled by his jacket.

'The marshal? He did something to harm you?'

'He tried to have his way.' She pulled her face back and looked up at him, her grey eyes glazed with tears. 'It was such a surprise, Johnny. I thought him such a well-mannered man.'

Johnny allowed a small smile to play on his lips at her naïvety. 'He's a stone-killer, Joanna. That's what he does. It's his life. On top it's all gentility and politeness but underneath lives another creature.'

'Well,' she sniffled, 'I am a wretched thing and a fool. I felt . . . I don't know . . . how could he expect that of me? It was only the immobility of his wounded arm that saved me, I think it is worse than he says.'

For a brief second Johnny relished her closeness to him, the warmth of her body pressed against him and the tears wet on his shoulder. He wanted nothing more at that moment than to spend the rest of his life protecting her.

'If you'll allow me, Joanna,' he whispered, 'I'll care for you.'

She looked up at him, her eyes mellowing as she understood the full meaning of what he was saying. Behind the tears a glow of softness began to form and she sighed contentedly, her eyes closing softly as he sought her lips with his.

'I didn't know,' she sighed as they

parted. 'I hoped . . . but I didn't know for sure.'

'Didn't know what?' he asked.

'That you cared so, of course.'

'Why, Joanna,' he grinned shyly, 'my heart has been aching for you ever since we first met.'

'Then why didn't you say something, you silly thing?'

He hunched his shoulders in embarrassment. 'I'm just an ignorant man. I didn't feel good enough.'

She pulled him close again. 'You are more than good enough.' And they kissed once more.

The two of them walked out that day, forgetting all lessons. She with her arm in his, boldly for all to see. It made Johnny's heart sing with delight as they made their way up through the higher town and into the countryside beyond. Here, free of the bustling streets below, they sat surrounded by carpets of wild gentian and columbine scattered in sweet grass beneath the dappled shade of a maple tree. They talked and kissed and began to discover all there was to know about each other.

From their vantage point the western Rocky Mountains were clear, rising rugged and grey on the horizon with hazy forests of aspen climbing the lower slopes beneath a blue sky free of even a single cloud. Meadowlarks sang and quivering painted lady butterflies fluttered from flower to flower searching out nectar. It seemed to Johnny as if the world had suddenly opened up for him. He told Joanna everything about himself, it poured out as if the cork had been removed from a bottle. His parents' death and the unfortunate separation of himself and his brothers. His running away and being mistakenly imprisoned for the murder of Preacher Inx, his escape and all of his subsequent adventures.

She listened attentively, by turns clutching a hand to her breast or covering her mouth in dismay. When he had finished, she laid her hand over his where it rested on the grass.

'My, what a life you have had. So much hardship and injustice. Poor Johnny.' Her fingers played softly across his face cupping his cheek. 'My own is so different. Caring parents and a loving home. Careful studies and contentment. I feel you have been cheated so.'

Johnny broke off a long stem of grass and placed it between his teeth as he stared off towards the distant mountains. 'It is as it is, I guess. You play the cards you're dealt.'

'Well,' she said, getting to her knees and enfolding him in her arms. 'I shall hold you close from now on for I believe I love you truly, Johnny Dollar.'

'Then you'd best be calling me by my right name. It's John Cable.'

19

Johnny walked tall now. He felt renewed in energy; with Joanna by his side he believed he could cast off for ever the suffocating cloak of his past, or at least face it with determined confidence. But as so often happens at such times, there sidles in a slinking black dog from out of the shadows, a feral beast only too ready to throw sand in the eyes of the hopeful.

It began when Johnny decided to face up to Marshal Slade and call him to task for attempting to take Joanna's virtue. A wild move for such a young man, to stand up to a proven killer. So, it must be said that on the chosen day he approached the marshal's office with some degree of trepidation.

Jack Slade was sitting at ease in a round-backed swing-chair, feet up on his desk and surrounded by three of his new deputies. They appeared casual and friendly types on the face of it, but each bore some mark of his true profession. It was impossible to miss. The way a six-shooter was low slung, a knife scar running down a cheek, even just the way a man stood. But mostly it was an air about the men, a certain tense readiness that said these were professionals, not any casual labourers.

'Why, hello there, Johnny,' Slade greeted him in a cheerful manner. 'How goes it?'

'I'd like to speak with you, Marshal.'

'Sure, Johnny, sure. Say your piece.'

'It's a personal matter. Can we have a moment?'

Slade swung his boots down and looked around at his watchful companions. 'Fellers,' he said. 'This here is Johnny Dollar. Young man that saved me from getting a knife in the neck. He looks meek enough, don't he? But come the moment he let fly with that shotgun without a second's thought. You all say howdy.'

The men grunted a chorus of greeting, looking at Johnny with slightly different and more speculative eyes.

'My new deputies, Johnny. I know them one and all. These are good men to have in your corner when a fight is on and I need them by me now. This here town is growing by the day. It will need a strong arm to keep the law safe here. Now,' he said, rising and wincing slightly as he slipped his stiff gun arm into the sling he wore. 'Let's you and me walk a while and discuss this matter of yours.'

Johnny noticed that the marshal now wore a second firearm on the opposite side to his normal cross-draw pistol. He wondered whether the lawman had lost some of the edge with his right hand since the knife had cut into his shoulder.

They left the office together and walked the boardwalks of the upper town. Along the way, Slade doffed his hat politely to passing womenfolk with a pleasant, 'Good day, ma'am,' or greeted some dignitary with a 'Morning, Councillor. How goes it this fine day?' Even the store-tenders were given friendly recognition. 'Zeb, you and your boy going fishing soon? You count me in, you hear?'

'Good folks these, Johnny,' he observed as they walked. 'Be a great town some day with good cash money to be made by all. Now, what's this pressing matter of yours?'

Johnny drew a deep breath, 'It's about Miss Joanna, Marshal,' he began.

'Uhuh,' said Slade noncommittally.

'She and I are walking out now.'

'Well, that's fine, Johnny. I'm real pleased for you. You'll make a fine pair,' Slade grinned good-naturedly.

'She told me what happened the other night and I don't take kindly to that sort of thing.'

Slade halted a moment and looked crestfallen. Rubbing his chin with his good hand he spoke soberly.

'Yeah, I'm right sorry about that, Johnny. I hope you ain't about to call me out for that little slip of the proprieties there.'

'Well,' Johnny said doubtfully, not expecting this sort of response. 'I just want you to know I won't abide any of that kind of behaviour in the future.'

'You're right, Johnny. It was real wretched of me. Please, you must say to Joanna that the devil took hold of me that evening. She's a damn fine lady, Johnny and normally I wouldn't wish a hair on her head harmed. Tell the truth, I don't know what came over me. I was just . . . well, I don't know how to explain it, I'm ashamed to say that some carnal beast was let loose that night.' Slade looked down at the shining toes of his polished boots. 'Please offer her my heartfelt apologies. I hope you'll accept them too.'

It should be understood that the nature of such a man as Jack Slade was ambiguous to say the least. He was, like many lawmen, capable of great charm and civility, a veneer that masked a willingness to commit bloody murder without remorse, an ability that lurked all too readily not far below the surface. In any other time he would be considered a dangerous psychopath, with this outward urbanity veiling deadly cruelty, but in these days he was a useful compliment to society. As long as he served on the side of law and order where his murderous tendencies could be given full rein without reprimand he was to be considered an upright and valued member of frontier society. So it was that, whilst on the one hand he would have no qualms about beating a man to death with a blunt instrument, with a swing of the pendulum his manner could alter to that of warm and companionable friendship.

'I appreciate what you're doing here, Johnny,' Slade went on. 'Took some guts to come see me like this. Now, for the sake of our friendship I hope we're all square on this?'

Johnny looked doubtful; he was a little confused by this kind of contrite response, a thing that he had not in the least expected.

'Will you shake on it, Johnny?' Slade asked, holding out his good left hand.

'I will.' Johnny said, looking Slade straight in the eye and shaking the offered hand. 'We're all square.'

'Well,' said Slade briskly. 'Now that's out of the way, there's something I want to talk to you about, Johnny Dollar. I need good men around me, men I can trust, so I'm going you offer you the full-time position of town deputy. Proper and above board, all signed and sealed, legal like. You get three hundred dollars a month and keep, I'll supply ammunition, you bring your own firearms. The town council has given me the budget to do it, they see how it is here and want to keep the town clean so it can grow. It's true we need the labours of those unruly fellows in the town below but we have to keep them in order. What do you say, Johnny? Be a nice way for you to make a tidy sum if you're serious about setting up house with Miss Joanna.'

'Oh, I'm right serious on that score,' said Johnny as he thought the proposal over. It seemed an excellent offer, a way of providing for himself and Joanna and giving her all the best he could hope for. 'I'll do it,' he said a moment later.

'Good thinking.' Slade grinned, his eyes twinkling as he slapped Johnny on the back. 'One thing, though.' He leant forward close to Johnny's ear, his eyes suddenly sharp and voice cold as ice. 'You know that if you had called me out here in the street, I'd have put one in your head before you'd even cleared leather. You know that, don't you?'

It was an obvious warning, Johnny could not avoid but understand: Slade would let it ride this time but he was not to think that any other similar criticism would be treated with such urbanity.

'I know it,' Johnny allowed.

'Right,' said Slade, returning quickly

to his former cheerful self. 'Then let's get us along to a lawyer and have you sworn in and contracted up all proper then.'

20

So, Johnny became a town policeman. He bought himself a new outfit with his first month's wages to celebrate the position: a red waistcoat to show off the tin badge of office that he wore pinned to his chest, and a pair of striped pants, with a set of kid gloves to match. He kept his round-topped flat-brimmed hat and bearskin coat against cold days and felt a real dandy as he patrolled the streets of the lower town. Joanna was pleased to see him looking so fine, she was proud of his advancement and told him so. It gave them both a respected position amongst town society, and those in the upper town smiled on them with approval and wished the young couple well.

They were married that spring. It was a quiet affair, with only a few others present, Johnny's one regret that day being the absence of Gunny. The old man had gone to ground somewhere in the lower town and Johnny had not been able to find him anywhere. The knot tied, Johnny carried Joanna off to the house he had rented at the lower end of the upper town and they settled in to a blissful few months of tender happiness. The honeymoon over, Johnny tied on his six-gun and went back to his job as town deputy and Joanna to hers in the schoolroom.

As time passed Johnny learnt much of his new trade from the other deputies. How to see the intentions of an opponent, to watch the movement of a man's eyes. How to strike before a gun is drawn, to cut in on instinct and worry about the right or wrong of it later. Better an opponent laid low than a bullet in your brain. To keep your distance if it came to a fight, the better to see the peripherals, for you could never know who backed up the offender you faced. How to deal with loud mouthed drunks and spiteful cot girls toting long needle-sharp hatpins. To keep an even-minded cool-headed detachment when in the midst of flying bullets. All were lessons he learned, some of them the hard way and others through good advice.

During all this new activity though it was the sight of Gunny's decline that troubled him the most. On his rounds he would often see the old-timer, the man's features now wasted away to skin and bone from their earlier healthy ruddiness, when he rode the wind-blasted box up on the stage. Johnny saw a shadow of a drunk, slipping surreptitiously around the fringes of crowded saloons, cowed and beaten by the changes in his circumstances. He hated to see it and often slipped the old man a few dollars, knowing full well that it probably went only on more whiskey rather than a decent meal. He protected Gunny where he could but often came across his beaten figure laid out supine in a dark alleyway, the face bruised and cut.

If he had been able, Johnny would have taken the old man in, but, in some desperate show of half-remembered pride, Gunny denied all offers of such help.

Jack Slade also prospered, apparently growing with the town. He bought property and started a haulage company, soon becoming an affluent elected member of the town council whilst still retaining his position as marshal.

Of his brothers, Johnny heard little. There was the occasional report received of some train robbery but always at a distance, for which Johnny was grateful. He had no wish to have to face them in his position as deputy; he felt the ethics of such a problem would be beyond him.

Julesville had grown. It now possessed over 200 houses and more than thirty shops; there was even the prospect of an opera house. Enough money passed through the burgeoning town to justify the opening of three banks, though this brought a new set of problems. It necessitated transporting cash in large quantities; this in turn attracted the unwanted attention of road agents as a honeypot attracts flies. It soon became clear that the town's police force would have to extend its services beyond the town limits if they were to protect Julesville's economy. The deputies had a hard time of it and long hours were spent not only patrolling the streets but also riding guard with the bullion-loaded wagons, which were often carried under the auspices of Slade's haulage company. It meant that Johnny had less time to spend with Joanna and this distressed both of them. Luckily Joanna had her schooling to occupy her, which kept her busy; even so the young couple missed each other's company.

A shift occurred, it seemed to Johnny; something changed not only in his own personal affairs but also in the developing nature of the town. On the surface all appeared well as more of the Frontier roughness disappeared, streets became cleaner and quieter and the upper town took on a more peaceful and prosperous air. But Johnny sensed that below the surface a different force was at work, something to do with the affluence and the air of greed that accompanied it. A perversion of justice crept in, one that favoured the wealthy and ignored the ills of the poorer members of the community. He could see how the inhabitants of the upper town became sleeker and smugger, secure in all that their wealth could provide. It was an uncomfortable sensation and it scratched at Johnny like a thorn in a blanket. Even, he noticed much to his dismay, Lassiter's Eureka Loophole took on an air of respectability as its owner moved his household to the upper town and bought a two-storeyed brick-built town house. The fat, it seemed, prospered whilst the lower-town inhabitants kept their lowly status and little was done to improve their situation or their environment. They were merely the teeming worker ants, fit only to supply the rich with gain won by the products of the ill-rewarded labour of the poor.

Such an imbalance could not last.

21

Johnny was woken in the early hours by a pounding at his door. He was dead tired and it was quite a time before he could bring himself to get up and answer.

'What is it?' asked Joanna sleepily.

'I'll see to it,' he said, sliding out of bed and stepping into his long john. 'Go back to sleep, honey.'

Muttering curses and with a pistol in his hand, he made his way towards the continuing hammering.

'What?' he growled irritably as he swung the front door open. 'What is it now?'

There was a small boy there, a ragamuffin of a fellow who stepped back nervously.

'You Deputy Dollar?' he asked in a querulous voice.

'I am, what do you want at this hour?'

'You're to come right off. Missy Jane sent me, it's Gunny Debreau,' the boy said.

Johnny had no idea who Missy Jane was but he could see from the boy's urgency that something must be badly wrong.

'Wait there,' he said. 'I'll go get dressed.'

The boy led him through the darkened streets down to the lower town, along filthy alleyways until they came to a cot house amongst the gloom of the overhanging buildings. A wooden sign hanging at an angle outside proclaimed it was the 'Joy Palace', although Johnny considered there was nothing in the least joyful about the place. Feral dogs growled over scraps at the doorway and the boy fearlessly kicked them away before opening the flap. It was a long, narrow, tented structure, dark inside with blanketed divisions separating the cots where the girls carried out their trade.

The boy pointed to the further

reaches. 'Missy Jane's up the end there.'

Johnny hurried along the dark corridor. Mumblings and the loud sound of snoring arose on either side. A woman sat at the far end, a candle alight on a folding table before her. She was an immense creature, her features flaccid and appeared unnaturally waxen in the candlelight. She wore a blowsy, ruffled nightdress that covered her bulk from head to toe. Her fingers were covered with rings that glittered in the candle glow and she was polishing her fingernails daintily with a buff.

'You the deputy?' she asked, not looking up.

'I am,' said Johnny.

'There's an old-timer over there.' She waved a fat finger to a ragged bundle in the corner of the tent. 'Says he knows you.'

Johnny went over and knelt down. He turned the unconscious figure of Gunny over.

'He ain't dead yet,' said Missy Jane.

'But close enough. Run foul of Lash Lassiter.'

Gunny hung limp as Johnny lifted the frail figure in his arms. 'What happened?' Johnny asked.

'Can't say,' said the woman. 'I know Gunny though. He's a good fellow, he wouldn't have started anything,' she went on. 'He didn't deserve that kind of handling.'

'Thank you kindly for caring for him.'

The big woman shrugged. 'Like to do more for him but I got a business to run here.'

Johnny turned to the boy still waiting at the tent entrance. 'Son, go fetch the doctor. Bring him to my house right quick, there's a silver dollar in it if you run fast.'

Johnny carried Gunny out of the tent and climbed the hill back up to his quarters. Gunny weighed next to nothing; Johnny had carried children who weighed more. The old man's body was thin and sticklike, the skin stretched tight over his bones. Johnny could feel dampness under his hands coming from the tattered shirt on Gunny's back. When he got inside and laid Gunny on his parlour couch he could see that his hands were covered in blood.

Gunny groaned as Johnny brought water to his lips. His eyes fluttered and opened.

'That you, Johnny?' he asked breathlessly.

'It is, old man. What happened to you?'

Gunny crinkled his weathered lips bitterly and drew a deep breath. 'There's more going on here than you know,' he whispered.

Johnny gave him some more water. The old man swallowed and writhed painfully.

'Take heed of Lassiter,' he said. 'I overheard them talking. He's in it with the others . . . '

'Who? What do you mean, Gunny?'

But it was no use, the old man had

slipped into unconsciousness again. There was a knock on the front door and Johnny let the doctor in, flicking a coin at the waiting boy who ran off with a nod of thanks.

'What's this?' asked the doctor, bustling in.

'The old man there, he's in a bad way, Doc. You do your best for him, no matter what it costs.'

'I do my best anyway, Deputy,' grunted the doctor proudly.

'Sure,' said Johnny. 'No offence intended. Just see him right, will you?'

Half an hour later, Johnny was standing fretting by the parlour door waiting impatiently whilst the doctor finished up. Joanna stood beside him in her dressing gown, her arm looped through his and a worried expression on her face.

'Those are severe whip marks across his back. He's been lashed pretty bad and it's not the first time,' the doctor said, wiping his hands on a towel. 'I've dressed them as best I can but the old fellow needs feeding up; he's in a bad way. Half starved, in fact. Too much drink, I'd say, at his age; he should be taking it easy, not drowning himself in whiskey.'

Johnny nodded. 'I know it, but he ain't one to listen.'

'Can you care for him here? The bandages need changing regular. I'll leave some ointment to put on the abrasions. Mostly, though, get some good meat broth down him and keep him drinking clean water. He's tough; he'll pull through with proper care.'

'We'll get it done.' Joanna promised firmly.

'I'm grateful to you, Doc,' said Johnny.

'Deputy,' said the doctor, sighing as he sadly, shrugged on his jacket, 'I see it each and every day in this town.'

When the doctor had gone, Joanna and Johnny sat beside Gunny's made-up bed on the couch. Joanna's head lay on Johnny's thigh as she drifted off to sleep again and he placed an affectionate arm protectively around her shoulder. Silently he looked at the shrunken old man, who lay sleeping, mouth agape, looking more like a dead man than a live one in the pale lamplight. There was something of a lost father in the man for Johnny and, despite Gunny's fall from grace, Johnny could not but help loving the old man. He felt the fury slowly beginning to rise in his chest at thought of all that Gunny had suffered; it crept up his body in a fiery vein until the prospect of beating Boss Lassiter to a bloody pulp filled his brain with a pulsing red light.

22

Gradually, over the next few days, Gunny began to show signs of improvement. He was not coherent, still thrashing in the nightmare of his whiskey addiction and the effects of the brutal beating. The positive thing about the situation was that, in his weakened state, Gunny was unable to move from his bed and therefore indulge his craving for liquor.

Joanna nursed him tenderly and with Johnny's help the two of them bathed and cleaned the raw lash marks and encouraged food to pass between the wrinkled lips. Gunny was sick often; there was no way that a withdrawal from his constant supply of alcohol would be an easy passage. With a patience that impressed Johnny no end, Joanna tended to the old man compassionately and without the least hint of anger. It only deepened his devotion to her as he watched her bathe Gunny's fevered brow and spoonfeed him from a bowl.

'You are something else, darlin',' he said as he watched, so quietly that she almost did not hear him. She turned and smiled softly at him, then blew him a kiss.

Later that morning Johnny went to see Jack Slade.

Slade was agitatedly giving out instructions and barely noticed as Johnny entered the town marshal's office. 'Johnny,' he finally greeted after he had sent two deputies on their way.

Their relationship had been maintained solely on a professional basis, neither engaging with the other in any social activities apart from those required at town functions, and then only for politeness's sake. It suited them both. Johnny, for his part, still could not quite forget the unpleasant approaches made to Joanna by the marshal. Slade, who was a loner at the best of times, preferred to maintain his status as a man apart.

'What's up?' asked Johnny.

'We've been hit again,' Slade said bitterly. 'Another bank coach gone. Damn it! They always seem to know when we're making a big-cash run. Driver and guards killed. The coach found in some gully, with the team run off.'

'Any idea who it is?'

'My guess is that Hellblazing crew. They're back in the Territory I'm thinking.'

Johnny's heart sank; it was a situation he had not wanted to occur again.

'There's something I want to talk to you about,' he said, partly to change the subject and get away from the unpleasant thoughts of his brothers.

'Uhuh,' Slade grunted, his eyes fixed on the paperwork that lay scattered on his desktop.

'It's about Lassiter.'

Slade looked up and tilted his head questioningly.

'He's set about my old partner, Gunny Debreau. Near beat the old man to death with that whip of his.'

'So?' asked Slade.

'I mean to take him to task about it. I'm just letting you know beforehand.'

Slade scratched his chin and shrugged coolly. 'Guess that's your affair, Johnny. Though the way I heard it, old Gunny is a worthless drunk now. He's dug his own hole.'

'That's as may be,' said Johnny. 'But he was my partner and there's no way he deserved what Lassiter did to him. I mean to make him pay, with or without your blessing.'

A curtain seemed to descend over Slade's face. A blankness that hid his thoughts. He got up suddenly and looped his twin-pistol gunbelt around his waist, fastening the buckle with a quick tug.

'OK, Johnny,' he said. 'Let's you and me go see Mr Lassiter. You tend to your business and I'll see you're not interrupted.'

The two of them left the office and walked side by side down towards the lower town. Along the way, Slade continued his normal polite greetings to all and sundry, yet Johnny knew the man well enough now to detect a certain tenseness in him.

The Eureka Loophole was pretty near empty when they entered, the mining crews away on the day shift. Only a lone bartender polished glasses and a few determined night-long gamblers still played off in a gloomy corner. Sunlight streamed in through the batwing door and cast beams filled with dust motes like the swirl of a myriad of tiny pale flies. The vinegary taint of stale liquor, which seemed to exude from every beam and plank of the place, steeped the saloon in a dank atmosphere that even the sunlight could not dispel.

Lassiter stood leaning over the bar with his back to them; a hefty ledger open before him. He licked at a pencil stub and, adding on his fingers, made numerical notes in the book; occasionally he took a drink from a schooner of beer standing beside his elbow. He turned at the creaking clatter of the twin doors and saw the two men only as black silhouettes against the bright sunlight. Lassiter hooked his thumb in the rolled whip at his waist.

'Morning, gents,' he said. 'What's your pleasure?'

'No pleasure at all,' said Johnny, stepping forward.

'Oh, it's you, Deputy,' said Lassiter slyly. 'And who's that with you?' His face changed slightly as he recognized Slade. 'Marshal. What d'you want here?'

'Nothing,' answered Slade coolly. 'You could say I'm just observing.'

Lassiter lowered his head, his chins pressed down on his chest as he glowered at them. 'What's this about?'

'It's about Gunny Debreau,' said Johnny, slowly beginning to take off his jacket.

'That old bum,' snorted Lassiter.

'What's his problem now?'

'His problem is that you near beat him to death,' said Johnny. He folded his jacket neatly and hung it over the back of a chair. 'Now I'm about to oblige you with the same.'

'That a fact?' Lassiter grinned confidently. 'Well,' he said, easing himself away from the bar. 'You've wanted this a long time, haven't you, Deputy? So let's see what you've got.'

His hand dropped to his waist and slipped the bullwhip free from its binding, the long leather uncoiling with a rattle like a black snake on the wooden floorboards at his feet.

Johnny unbuckled his gunbelt and had begun to place it over his jacket when the whip shot out with a venomous crack, the flying end travelling faster than sound and erupting the air next to Johnny's head as it whipped the hat off his head.

There was the squeak of moving chairs as the gamblers turned quickly at the sound. Slade turned to face them.

He parted the front of his jacket and exposed the two holstered pistol grips. 'Private matter, gents,' he said calmly. 'You just carry on with your game.' He moved away from the bar.

'Come on then,' Lassiter said cockily to Johnny as the two of them circled each other. 'The likes of you ain't up to me, gun-toting deputy or not,' he sneered.

Johnny crouched, waiting for the expected lash. But Lassiter was quick, faster than could be expected of such an overweight character. He disguised his movement and the whip end flicked out. It caught Johnny high on the brow just above the eye. The sting was sharp and sudden and Johnny's eye filled with moisture as he felt blood trickle down his face from the split skin.

'Going to open you up like a ripe pumpkin,' Lassiter promised gleefully.

Lassiter was right-handed and Johnny instinctively moved left in an attempt to make it harder for Lassiter to raise his whip hand. Then Johnny snatched up a chair and held it before him as he advanced quickly, hoping to catch Lassiter unawares and reduce the whip length between them. But Lassiter adroitly shuffled sideways and, with a high looping spin of the bullwhip, caught the legs of the chair in the coiling leather and ripped it from Johnny's hand.

He chuckled and Johnny remembered that laugh from Gomar, the same laugh he had given as he pummelled Johnny on the head with the whip stock.

The lash spun out again and caught Johnny across the back, slashing open his shirt. Johnny gasped at the stinging pain that burned like a hot iron.

'You like that?' jeered Lassiter evilly, enjoying Johnny's cry of pain. Sweat was breaking out on his brow as he swung his arm above his head, his eyes wide, with the whites showing wildly. He delivered another mighty blow that cracked in the air as it bit into Johnny's arm, ripping open the sleeve from shoulder to elbow.

The pain was intense and Johnny struggled to forget it as he looked for an opening that he could make to close with Lassiter. Once inside his reach, Johnny knew that only then would they be on an even footing. He clutched at his arm and felt the blood trickling through his fingers as he continued to circle.

'Going to be more of that,' assured Lassiter, swinging again. Johnny leapt back as the lash snapped out across his neck and he felt his back colliding heavily with the bar behind him. He reached out to steady himself and his fingers touched the schooner of beer that Lassiter had left there. In one motion he caught up the glass and threw it all into Lassiter's face.

Lassiter spluttered, blinking as the beer temporarily blinded him. Johnny leapt forward and grasped Lassiter's whip hand at the wrist. He pulled it aside and delivered a deep sweeping uppercut that threw the fat man's chins back with a resounding smack. Lassiter staggered away, dazed, the whip slipping from his fingers. Johnny waded in. Now things were even and he took his time, the months of tuition on the wild streets of the lower town paying off as he picked his spot and delivered blow after hard blow against Lassiter's yielding bulk. Unfairly, Johnny dropped his bunched fist and hit Lassiter below the waistline of his pressed pants. The fat man doubled over with an anguished, keening cry, Johnny hit the side of his exposed head with a downward chop.

Lassiter fell to his knees, raising his hands protectively over his head. 'OK, OK,' he cried. 'I've had enough.'

Johnny ignored his pleas, the memory of the man as prison guard and of his mistreatment of Gunny was roaring through his blood.

'Maybe you have, but I haven't.' Johnny snatched up the fallen bullwhip. 'How'd you like a taste yourself,' he said, snaking the whip through the air and cracking a blow across Lassiter's back.

Lassiter screamed as the lash hit his fat shoulders. Johnny delivered another blow and Lassiter fell over, a quivering blood-stained heap lying in a foetal pose on the floor. Johnny stepped over him, the wildness of vengeance running through him. He raised his hand to bring down the reinforced stock hard against the fallen man's temple but Slade stepped in and locked his wrist in a strong grip.

'Enough, Johnny. He's had enough.'

Johnny stood there panting, his eyes staring. After some moments he steadied himself and stood up, allowing the whip to drop from his hand.

'You . . . you . . . ' cried Lassiter, looking up at him in terrified dismay from a crumpled face. Tears streaked his bloodied chin and one eye was already puffing into a bruised ball. His split lips sagged and spittle and blood dribbled over his jaw. 'You!' he cried, pointing an accusing finger. 'I know who you are now . . . I recognize you. You're Cable. Johnny Cable!' he screamed. 'Escaped from Gomar pen, killing guards and men as you went.'

Johnny did not hesitate, he swung his foot and booted Lassiter in the jaw, felling the man, cutting him short as he fell into unconsciousness.

'Cable?' frowned Slade. 'You're a Cable, Johnny? One of the Cable brothers? Tell me it ain't true.'

Johnny looked at him, his nostrils flaring with spent fury; he no longer cared. Not what Slade or anybody else thought. 'Yes,' admitted. 'I'm a Cable. I don't run with them or have anything to do with them but they're my brothers all right.'

'Hell, Johnny,' gasped Slade, his face a picture of confusion. 'How come you never told me this?'

'To what point, Marshal? I left my brothers and that life behind me years ago.'

Slade chewed at his lip thoughtfully for a long moment, then he raised his eyebrows. 'I guess we all have something best forgotten. I ain't better than the rest on that score.' He admitted it with surprising honesty. 'Thing is, Johnny, with the Hellblazers hitting the bank coaches we have a problem. Folks are going to think it mighty strange, with you being their brother and all.'

'You think I let on when one's due to make a run, is that it?'

Slade shook his head. 'I don't think that for a minute, Johnny. I've known you too long now. But it's not what I think, it'll be with the town council that you'll have a problem.'

'But you're on the council. You can put them straight.'

Slade shook his head doubtfully. 'Sure, but I'm only one man. The others might think different. If it comes to a vote, who knows? You could be out on your ear. Think on it, boy. How does it sound? An escaped con with a murder charge hanging over him and brothers in one of the worst gangs we've seen around here for years. What would you think?'

Johnny had to admit the force of it when it was put like that. His shoulders sagged and the smart of his stinging wounds suddenly pressed in on him. He winced, picking at the torn edge of his blood-soaked shirtsleeve.

'You get along and get yourself cleaned up. I'll see what I can do in the meantime,' Slade promised. 'You,' he said, turning to the bartender. 'Get your boss seen to and make sure you keep your mouth shut about all you heard here.' Slade knew, even as he said it, that it was an idle hope and that the news would be all over the town by afternoon.

Slade toed the fallen heap of Lassiter with a look of disdain. 'Met your match there all right, didn't you, fat boy?'

23

Gunny was more able now and he managed to sit up on the couch and watch Johnny as he washed the whip marks with a bowl of water he'd brought in and set on the parlour table. The old man was still frail but his skin showed a healthier colour now and most of the rheumy discolouration had left his eyes. Joanna was at her lessons so the two of them were left alone in the house.

'What you been getting into?' he asked as Johnny shed his torn shirt and started gingerly to clean away the blood.

'Bit of a disagreement,' Johnny answered evasively.

'Not on my account, I hope.'

Johnny stopped bathing his wounds and looked across at him. 'Now why on earth would I want to do a dumb thing like that?'

'I don't know,' grumbled Gunny. 'You took me in here, your beautiful wife's been taking care of me. I thought maybe you and Lassiter . . . ' he left the rest to hang in the air.

Johnny nodded, padding at his arm again with a damp cloth. 'He won't bother you again.'

'I knew it!' hissed Gunny angrily. 'You've been stepping in and taking my part, haven't you? Getting yourself into trouble on my account. Why'd you do that?'

'Because you're a damned old nuisance, is why. Now shut up and let me see to these scratches, will you?'

'Here,' Gunny snapped. Clad only in his long johns, he got to his feet and crossed over. 'Let me do it. Darn it, Johnny, you should have stayed away from that one. He's mean as they come and won't let it rest.'

'Then that'll be all the excuse I need to finish it permanent,' answered Johnny coldly.

Gunny dabbed quietly at the weals

on Johnny's back for a moment, 'Got you a few good ones here,' he observed after a bit.

'You should know.'

'That's true,' agreed Gunny with a grunt. 'I overheard him this time. He's into something big. Something I shouldn't have been close enough to hear about.'

'What? What did you hear?'

'I was sweeping out back of the bar, as I'm supposed to. Lassiter was speaking real low with someone behind a curtained-off storeroom they've got there. I couldn't see who he was talking to; two or three people maybe. But old Lassiter was being very cautious in his conduct, I know that. Like he was a little afraid, you know? It was a plan of sorts. 'You come here', 'We do that', those kinds of phrases. I did hear one of them say . . . 'Timing is everything' . . . but that's all I got.'

'Any ideas?' asked Johnny.

'Not really, I didn't recognize any voices. Suddenly Lassiter whips back the curtain and sees me there. Then he gets all angry and starts beating on me. Asking who I'm spying for. The man was in a pure rage, almost out of control. Didn't take long before that long bullwhip was out. I don't remember much about it after that.'

Johnny stood up, shaking his head. 'I'd like to know who he was cooking this up with.' His thoughts roamed to his outlaw brothers and the robbed bullion coaches; he prayed that they were not involved. 'It has to be the gold shipments. The only thing of real value going in and out of here.'

'They got any big movements of cash due at the moment?' asked Gunny.

'Nothing out of the ordinary as far as I know.'

'Well, best keep your ear to the ground and watch out for one coming up.'

Johnny gazed out of the window into the distance. 'Not sure if that's going to be possible. Lassiter recognized me during our little set-to, blurted my name and that made the connection with my brothers and the Hellblazing Gang. Slade's pretty sure it's been them that's hitting the shipments. Could be the town council will kick me out of office as being too much of a risk.'

'That's too bad, Johnny.'

Johnny shrugged. 'What can you do?'

24

The three main controllers of the Julesville banks sat in the town's new town hall offices, the walls already festooned with freshly stuffed deer and buffalo heads. The floor was richly carpeted and fine bevelled oak panelling had been specially imported to create an atmosphere of staid conservative stability. Heavy curtains kept the hot sunlight outside the stained-glass windows and in the semi-gloom the three men sat at their ease, a decanter of the best French brandy between them.

'Are we prepared to risk it? That is the question,' said Carter F. Martin, the stocky, immaculately dressed eldest of the three. He wore a thick wiry brown beard that covered most of his chest like a bib, and was the sole owner of the Martin Mercantile Bank. He was perhaps the wealthiest of the three by quite a few thousand dollars.

'All our eggs in one basket,' said Jacob Short doubtfully; he was chairman of the board of the Julesville Dominion Bank. A soft, chubby, pink-faced character with an obvious liking for both the breadboard and the liquor cabinet.

The last member of the group was Caleb LeMay, a thin, pinched, sharp-featured man with all the nervous air of a worried accountant about to face a review of his books. Normally a Temperance Society supporter, he sipped at his brandy distastefully, only doing so as he was a little in awe of Carter F. Martin. Wrinkling his nose, he eventually pushed the glass aside.

'Might I have some water, do you think?' he asked. LeMay held a major controlling influence in the coalmine's own bank, known as the Julesville Coal Agency Bank.

'Of course,' grumbled Carter Martin distractedly. He rang a tiny service hand bell set on the table beside him.

A middle-aged servant dressed in a grubby white jacket and sporting unkempt hair answered the call almost immediately.

'Fetch some cold spring water for Mr LeMay, will you?' ordered Martin.

'Yessir, Mr Martin. Right off.' The man hurried away to do the banker's bidding and the three waited silently until he had returned with a jug, glass and napkin and placed it beside LeMay.

Martin took the opportunity to light a handsomely sized cigar; puffing a column of smoke he looked thoughtfully at the decorated ceiling.

'I believe all the risks are outweighed by the benefits, gentlemen.'

'You think so?' said Short, again doubtful.

'Yes. If we get the funds south in time we will surely make this a profitable killing. And double our investment easily,' replied Martin.

'Why not spread it over three or four transports though?' asked LeMay.

'Everything in one coach at such a time is surely a recipe for disaster.'

'I don't think so,' Martin puffed his cigar. 'Three or more coaches would only ensure attention and add to the delay.'

'Then why not three coaches but with only one of them carrying the load? Surely that would confuse any attempts by road agents?'

'It is impracticable. Remember we shall be travelling cross-country and not using normal stageline routes. The route will only be given out on the day and only I shall know it until then. As long as secrecy is maintained there is no way the villains will be aware of our intent.' Martin huffed impatiently. 'Gentlemen, we have held back on transport for over a month now. Our time is running out; we must act if this deal is to go through. Our vaults are filling up with gold coin and promissory notes are of no value for our project. Our partners need ready cash. Gunrunners are not the kind of men who will take paper; they want only gold.'

His two companions paused thoughtfully, weighing the prospect of even greater wealth against the possibilities of further raids by any outlaw gang.

'Heavily protected,' continued Martin, 'I'm sure we can guarantee safety. With Marshal Slade and his men plus the use of the reinforced Titan carriage as well, it is worth the gamble.' Martin pressed, obviously eager to make the deal.

Short and LeMay were swayed by Martin's overbearing confidence; one by one they slowly nodded their assent.

'A special run then, on the twenty-fourth of the month,' said Martin, fluffing his beard thoughtfully as he spoke. 'The Titan will be brought out of mothballs and fitted out for the trip. She'll be held in readiness under wraps at the livery stables. We'll run her south to the railhead and there our partners in the military can take over responsibility. They will lay on an army freight carriage to transport the gold to their contacts who will . . . how shall I put it . . . ' He paused enigmatically. 'Supply the hardware,' he finished with a slight smile of contentment. 'As to where the goods go from there we have no concern, except to be sure that we receive our share on arrival. My assumption is that they will be going to some South American dago fool with delusions of power and a self-seeking desire to create an army.'

'How do we excuse this unusual run to the marshal?' asked LeMay.

'We'll say it's new Federal Bank instructions; he's to be none the wiser. It'll be picked troops who meet the run, so it'll all look legitimate and above board when they get to the railhead.'

'And how can we be sure of receiving our share?' asked Short.

'Because, my dear friend,' said Martin in a condescending manner, 'my initial contact was through a certain high office in Washington. Nothing can go wrong with his backing. This acquaintance of mine needed very large sums to complete this deal; he has asked only those whom he knows he can trust implicitly to commit themselves to it. If there is any tomfoolery he will be brought down hard and he knows it.'

'So that we all understand each other,' butted in LeMay, 'each of us is about to embezzle the sum of three hundred and fifty thousand dollars from our banks' reserves and trust it to this venture. Am I correct? It is the same for each of us?'

'*Invest!*' said Martin sharply. 'Invest is the word. The money will be returned within a fortnight, doubled in value. Your accounts will balance again and each of us will have earned three hundred and fifty thousand clear and free, with no one being any the wiser.' He smiled thinly again: a smug, self-satisfied smile. 'It is perfect, my friends. Just perfect and we have no need to even move from our seats to make it happen.'

His pleasure would have been short-lived if he could have seen the lurking servant, who stood listening behind one of the heavy drapes hanging beside the entrance to the darkened room.

25

Three days later an uncomfortable-looking Marshal Slade came knocking on Johnny's door. Johnny showed him into the parlour and Slade, looking duly bashful, removed his hat and made his apologies to Joanna for the disturbance.

'You're out,' Slade said without further ado. 'Sorry, Johnny, but that's the way they see it. The town council voted on it and I've got to have your badge.'

Not surprisingly, Joanna was upset by this bluntness and the words tumbled angrily from her lips before she could hold them back. 'Even though there's not the slightest thing at all to link him with any wrongdoing?' she asked, staring daggers at Slade.

Slade sucked in his breath, 'I did all I could, I swear it. But they wouldn't budge. Believe me, I don't give it any credit. This is just the way of it.'

'How's it going to look?' asked Joanna, her face flushing. 'The whole town will say there's no smoke without fire. You're almost certainly tarring Johnny as an outlaw along with his brothers.'

Slade shook his head, looking across at a silent Johnny. 'That's not how I see it, Joanna. Anybody asks, anybody at all and I'll give Johnny a clean bill of health.'

Joanna just spat derisively. 'My husband's a good man, Marshal. He's been a loyal deputy to you and I believe this discredits this town, I really do.'

Johnny's gaze met Slade's evenly as he unfastened the badge from his waistcoat and handed it over.

'It gets worse,' said Slade.

Johnny jerked his head. 'Tell me.'

'They're talking of sending you back to the pen at Gomar.'

'I don't believe this,' cried Joanna. 'I really don't.'

'You going to do it?' asked Johnny.

Slade shrugged, 'It's the law. You've got a charge for murder to answer.'

'My Johnny's no murderer,' sobbed Joanna, clutching at Johnny's arm.

'He killed a man there, Joanna,' Slade explained. 'Another prisoner. I'm not talking about the preacher now, but an old trusty.'

Johnny sighed heavily. Once again his bad luck had followed him and found him out.

'If it hadn't been for that toad Lassiter,' Slade continued, 'no one would have known, but he's been bleating all over. Especially up there on the hill. The town council is having its hand forced; they can't ignore all the noise he's been making.'

Then, suddenly, the earth shifted beneath them with a sharp sideways jerk. All the house front windowpanes rattled nervously as if a thunderstorm was approaching from across the prairie. It was followed by a booming sound wave that was distant and muffled but rumbled up the hillside towards them ominously. The scream that came after it was clear enough, a high-pitched wailing, loud and jarring.

They all froze for a moment. Then Slade turned to the window as the scream came again.

'It's the mine!' he exclaimed.

All three ran to the front door and out on to the porch. There it was plain to see. A dark cloud rose in a billowing pillar a hundred feet high, from there it broke off and drifted east on a light top wind. The grey cloud smudged an ugly line on the bright sky and the steam whistle's scream of distress that followed it reached even into the comfortable parlours of the upper town above them. Its implications were all too plain.

'The mine!' breathed Johnny.

'God Almighty!' snapped Slade. He looked at Johnny. 'I'll need you, partner,' he said, tossing the badge back. 'Forget the council's stupidity. I'll need you now.'

'Oh, sure!' said Joanna disgustedly. 'When it comes to Johnny risking his life everything else is forgotten.'

'Leave it, Joanna,' Johnny said coolly. 'This comes first, the rest later.'

26

It had been planned well. The men who stood waiting knew it.

They had gathered casually, sitting on stoops or hanging around shop-fronts. Their ponies had been held in waiting readiness in shadowed alley-ways. To all who saw them they seemed to be innocent passers-by. Their leader, a man who spoke little, his scarred jaw seemingly locked tight by some accident that caused him to speak around gritted teeth, watched the plan come to fruition from beneath the brim of his round-topped hat. He still wore cavalry pants and moccasins but he no longer acted as a scout. The army had cast him out after the Freemantle shooting, deeming him unfit for service. No pension came his way, no show of gratitude for all his years of service, only a degrading resentment displayed by the whites for his accident of birth. In bitterness and poverty, Joey Tuppence had turned his back on accepted society and chosen instead a more rewarding way of life. This was his own plan, to be carried out now with military precision.

He had used his army training well in forming the plan, first scouting out the town, the layout of the banks and the presence of the mine. His inside man at the Town Hall offices had told him of the forthcoming transfer but had discovered nothing of the planned route the Titan gold coach would take. So, on his own initiative, Joey had decided that an alternative scheme had to be devised. One where the money was removed even before it was loaded on to the stagecoach.

He had discovered the key to his plot in the coalmine.

The coal around Julesville was surface-mined in strips. Once the surface layer of topsoil was removed and dug away the exposed coal seam below was excavated. Usually it was first blasted safely with black powder at the bottom of a forty-foot-deep trench, which was enclosed in a high bowl of earth left after the topsoil removal. But this had been a manufactured explosion that Joey had engineered, using a combination of both secretly installed barrels of powder and sticks of dynamite. The fire that ripped through the bench after the initial explosion was a lethal mix that dug deep into the friable coal and, unexpectedly fortunate for Joey, hit a hidden pocket of deadly firedamp gas.

The inflammable gas added its venom to the explosion that followed and the final smoke cloud was followed by a boiling sea of fire that spilled from the bench with such terrific force that men and beasts working there were tumbled like skittles in the shock wave. Rocks and debris loosened by the blast rose high in the air and rained down on the buildings of the lower town a quarter-mile away.

Stunned by the rolling blast wave, Johnny, Joanna and Slade, standing watching on the porch, staggered back unsteadily.

'They'll need the Black Maria down there,' said Slade decisively. Johnny knew about the Black Maria, it was a horse drawn van that served as both hearse and ambulance. Some said it had gained its name from a forceful Negress of awesome proportions called Maria Lee, who owned a boarding house in Boston, a woman whom the police often called on to handle difficult situations. Be that as it may, it was a direful-looking vehicle, the appearance of which usually presaged some awful disaster for the men at the mine.

'You get on down to the mine,' replied Johnny. 'I'll go get the van team hitched up.' He turned to Joanna. 'Find Gunny, tell him to meet me at the livery stables right off.' Slade looked across at him dubiously. 'He's the best damned driver I know,' explained Johnny. Slade nodded quick approval.

Joanna did not bother answering; she knew Gunny was fixing a warped window frame up at the schoolhouse and ran off to find him.

Slade's hand was on the pommel of his saddle and Johnny had started out into the street when they heard the first gunshots.

Both looked at each other, an unspoken query going between them as the boom of a double-barrelled shotgun reached them. 'Warning shots?' asked Johnny.

'No,' said Slade, who already knew of the plans for transporting the gold. 'It's a diversion at the mine. This has to be a raid. They're hitting the banks.'

'What do you want to do?'

'Quick, jump up behind,' Slade ordered as he mounted his horse. 'Let's get up to the office.'

As Johnny threw himself across the pony's flanks, Slade dug his heels in and the beast leapt forward, almost throwing Johnny off. They charged up the hill at the gallop, making for the marshal's office and scattering townsfolk who were already running down towards the mine. The screaming steam siren still blasted out its call and the rising noise of panic came from the crowded lower town. Scattered shooting followed them, although in the general pandemonium it was difficult to tell exactly where it came from.

Both men jumped down at the office door. The three other deputies stood on the sidewalk, already waiting there. Len Travis, Bill Wade and Charlie 'Bear Claw' Handy. Calmly and methodically, each was sliding shells into rifles and pistols as they prepared for Slade to give orders.

'Which bank?' Slade asked. 'Anybody know?'

'Sounds like all three,' answered the gloomy, lean-faced deputy called Len Travis, tossing a loaded Winchester in Johnny's direction.

'OK, we split up,' said Slade swiftly. 'Len, you and Charlie make for the Coal Agency. Johnny and Bill the

Dominion, and I'll take Martin's Mercantile. Come on now, let's do it, boys.'

Without hesitation the four deputies moved out at the run. Slade slipped his pistols from their holsters, slapped his horse aside and followed, checking the load as he ran.

'Good to have you back.' The deputy Bill Wade grinned at Johnny as they ran side-by-side, rifles held high. He was a good-natured block of a man with a brawler's face and broad shoulders; although on the surface he appeared to be as hard as nails there was a more considerate man underneath. Johnny had always enjoyed his company.

'Only for the duration,' Johnny supplied.

'Too bad, Johnny. That charge on you, it's bullshit all the way.'

'How do you want to do this?' Johnny asked as they approached the corner of an alley that let on to Main Street.

Main Street in Julesville was the dividing line between the upper and lower town terraces. It was a wide dusty street, one side occupied by a row of shops and private properties. The other, the lower side, fell away with a rough edged lip to form a crumbling step where the winter rains and heavy traffic had worn away the road margin. Below that the scattered slum of the lower town appeared on the hillside.

Both of them stately, brick-built structures, the Martin Mercantile and the Dominion Bank stood on Main Street separated by a hundred yards of properties crammed together; at the centre, a narrow side road led uphill to a junction where the squat, lesser favoured building of the Coal Agency Bank stood. It was a busy main street with work always in progress to stop the slippage downhill; deep trenches were often in place with large felled timbers laid out waiting to be buried in an attempt to reinforce the road. The road workers had fled along with many of the townspeople in answer to the screaming steam whistle. Horse-drawn flatbed carts and wagons stood parked, forgotten as the owners also ran to help out at the mine.

Joey Tuppence had been irritated to hear the gunfire start up, although he was not really that surprised. Whilst his plan had been conceived with military precision and with a desire for silence, his men were not disciplined soldiers.

They were a ragtag bunch of twelve men whom he had picked up from around the mountain badlands and beyond, from places he had come across in his time with the army. Some were hardened outlaws who he knew would handle the job efficiently; others though were more common chancers and rogues, some of them mentally unstable and not the brightest of specimens. He had guessed that the excitement would fire these types with an enthusiasm beyond their control and they would find it impossible not to let off their firearms. His main hope, though, had been that the distraction of the mine explosion would draw the townsfolk's attention away from the locality of the banks and in this he was fortunate, as the empty street proved.

Joey had three men at each bank, with another three holding each team's getaway horses nearby. His plan was to get the gold into specially reinforced large saddle-bags, as much as they could sensibly carry, to be taken on to a nearby meeting place outside the town where the heavy coinage would be transferred on to a flatbed wagon that would more easily carry it away at speed. There he would meet up with the instigator of the scheme and they would travel to a safe place to divide up the spoils.

Joey had expected the main body of the Julesville police force to go along with the rescuers but in this he was sadly mistaken.

Johnny and Bill Wade entered the empty Main Street and dashed across to the opposite side, where the broken edges of the eroded road offered them some cover. Slade, meanwhile, marched along the upper sidewalk in plain view, both pistols drawn and held high. The Mercantile Bank was the nearest and it was Slade's intended goal. Johnny and Wade could see the Dominion further down but its front was hidden by a collection of hanging signs advertising everything from Dentist to Shingle Maker.

'Will you look at him?' whispered Bill Wade, watching Slade with respectful awe. 'Bold as brass. Don't he beat all?'

Johnny snorted good naturedly. 'He does it every time. One day he'll get his fool head blowed off, going in like that.'

'Come on,' said Wade. 'Let's get on down to the Dominion before he starts raising Cain here and they know we're coming.'

Having said that the two hurried on, crouching low as they passed the Mercantile Bank front. A flurry of gunshots followed them, coming from further inside the town and the two men knew that the other deputies, Len and Charlie, had made contact with the raiders at the Coal Agency Bank.

'Sounds like it's started,' observed Wade.

Slade had reached the main door of the bank. Without hesitation he pushed the glass-panelled door open and strode inside. He saw the three armed men instantly, two of them masked and standing guard over the bank staff and the few customers; the other raider stood leaning over a clerk behind the counter as he nervously loaded heavy saddle-bags with gold coin from the safe.

Slade began firing, first from one pistol then the other as he advanced into the room.

The bank, a high-ceilinged large single room with open-topped counters, soon filled with powder smoke as Slade discharged his weapons. A raider tumbled, moaning wildly and clutching at his knee after the first few shots; his companion loosed off a couple of wild replies from his six-gun before he too succumbed to a chest wound and fell backwards in a spray of blood, landing on top of the crouching customers behind him. One of the customers screamed in anguish, staring in disbelief at the blood oozing from his side as he was wounded by Slade's indiscriminate gunplay.

Slade advanced steadily towards the counter, turning his attention to the last raider. The man was in a state of shock, unnerved and unprepared for the sudden turn of events. He raised both hands, in one was a pistol, the other was held up, palm open, in a restraining manner. Whether he was surrendering or warning Slade to come no further made little difference to the marshal, he fired his remaining bullets, missing with every one of them. Slugs whined off the top of the open safe door and shattered plaster from the wall behind it.

The raider stood there without firing, frozen, not twelve feet away, as Slade's hammers clicked on empty cylinders.

Grimly, Slade threw aside the two empty pistols; sweeping aside his coat tails he reached behind his back and brought out the back-up .44 stuffed in his belt. Still the raider made no move as Slade raised the pistol.

Their eyes met and the raider read the signs in Slade's cold stare. He began to whimper but Slade cut off his cries as he fired. The raider fell instantly, a neat hole drilled between his eyes. Whirling around, Slade held the .44 in both hands. His hands were trembling and he forced them to steady, lining up on the remaining wounded robber, who lay on his back on the floor, both hands clenched around his shattered knee. Slade fired, the raider coughed once, then lay still.

Slade stood still a long moment, his body quivering. Then, drawing a deep breath, he eased the tension and pushed the pistol back in his waistband.

'All right, folks,' he said. 'It's all over now.'

He had been temporarily deafened

by all the gunshots in the enclosed space; he did not realize that he had shouted loudly rather than offered the calming voice that he had intended. He was so deafened that he did not even hear the sentinel horse-tender, hiding in an alley with the getaway mounts, give up his post and pound desperately away.

27

Johnny and Wade were taken by surprise as they passed alongside a row of sutler wagons. The wagons, a gaudily painted species, much favoured by immigrants crossing the Rockies, had been pulled up in line ready to start their morning journey when the mine alarm had sounded.

It was from one of these that Joey Tuppence had seen Slade enter the Mercantile Bank. He had intended to oversee the two major bank robberies from there and he had cursed soundly as the rapid gunplay broke out from inside the Mercantile. He knew in a moment that the bank operation there was doomed, just from the way he'd seen Marshal Slade stride in so decisively with all the confidence of an experienced gunman. Even as he watched with exasperated contempt as the remaining horse-tender from the Mercantile rode past, making good a cowardly escape, he heard the scurrying sound of footsteps running alongside the wagons outside and guessed that other lawmen were making their way down towards the Dominion Bank.

He raised the canvas flap that covered the front of the wagon behind the driver's seat and he saw the stooped figures of Johnny and Wade hurrying past, rifles carried at the ready. Without a second's pause he drew his Navy Colt and fired at Wade's back, the bullet homing upon Wade's spine and killing him instantly.

As Wade fell forward his body became entangled with Johnny's feet in front of him and the two men fell heavily into the dust. Their fall saved Johnny from Joey Tuppence's second shot, which spurted dust in front of Johnny as he lay prostrate. He rolled sideways, dropping into cover over the edge of the crumbling road and falling into the ditch on the other side.

Cranking a shell into the Winchester's chamber, Johnny fired wildly over the lip of the ditch hoping to deter momentarily more shooting in his direction. He scooted along on his belly towards the sound of the last pistol shot, anticipating that his opponent in the wagon would find it more difficult to shoot down from behind the wagon sides. He risked a glimpse over the edge just in time to see Joey Tuppence's boots hit the hard-packed road on the other side of the wagon and make off towards the Dominion Bank.

Johnny was up in an instant; he leapt over the wagon tongue, which was at an angle in front of the wagon and took swift aim, bringing the rifle up to his shoulder. Joey was heading for a repair ditch and piled timbers that lay in the middle of the wide road as Johnny fired. The bullet hummed past Joey's ear. Right away he took evasive action, zigzagging and then diving behind the cover of the huge logs. There began a rapid firing session as Johnny backed away behind the safety of the wagon.

The Colt's heavy shells chewed holes in the woodwork of the wagon and plucked their way through the canvas sides. Tin pots clattered and china splintered as the bullets found their way into the household goods stored inside. It was awkward for Johnny to bring the long barrel of the rifle to bear so he laid it against a wagon wheel and drew his pistol. Then a hot shell plunked through the belly of a hanging oil lamp. The kerosene inside caught fire immediately and splattered a bloom of fire that rushed at the sun-baked canvas surrounding it. Above Johnny's head the wagon began to burn fiercely, the heat beating down on him.

The raiders inside the bank, their business completed, suddenly burst out on to the street. Joey began yelling at the three men to take cover and fire in Johnny's direction. A fusillade of shots poured at Johnny and he dropped backwards again, back into the ditch behind as bullets cut the air and spouted dust all around him.

He heard Joey call out, 'Bring up those horses, right now!'

As the sound of hoofbeats approached, Johnny risked another look over the edge and saw the raiders leaping up on to the swirling ponies. He crawled up, caught up his rifle again and he ran into the roadway.

Five men he counted as they laid on the spurs and sped off at breakneck speed. They were bunched together, one of them howling a wild cry of excitement as they galloped off down the street. The rifle bucked in his hands and one rider flipped over, falling across his horse's neck. A companion grabbed at him but the man slid from his grasp and fell away into the churned dust below.

Johnny stepped into the centre of the street as Slade came jogging up behind him. Johnny fired again after the departing raiders but the range was lost to him now and only dust hung in the air where the robbers had been.

'Where's Bill?' asked Slade. Johnny just shook his head in response.

'Damn!' cursed Slade. 'That's too bad. I liked old Bill. How many of them here?'

'There were five, I dropped one. He's up there, lying in the road.'

'Len's gone too,' Slade added sadly. 'Charlie says that two of them up at the Coal Agency made it away with cash. So that's seven of them on the run all told.'

'How much did they get away with?' asked Johnny.

'A pile,' answered Slade with a raised eyebrow. 'And we'd best get it back.'

'You're forming a posse then?'

Slade shook his head. 'No way we can round up enough men, everyone's down at the mine. No, we have to do this ourselves.'

'Three of us against seven,' Johnny said doubtfully.

There was a rumble behind them and they saw the strange sight of Gunny Debreau with 'Bear Claw' Charlie beside him up on the driving seat of the Titan stagecoach as it raced towards them.

'What th . . . ' gasped Slade.

'Climb aboard, gents,' called Gunny, pulling up beside him.

'We can't go chasing them in this,' snapped Slade.

'Why not?' said Gunny. 'We've six of the strongest pulling ponies you'll ever meet. And a reinforced coach with all the protection your hard head'll ever need. Get on, Marshal. Let's get it done.'

Slade looked across at Johnny, who only smiled and shrugged. 'You can't argue with this man,' he said. 'I've tried often enough and it ain't no good.'

With a faint look of indecision Slade opened the carriage door and climbed in.

'I'll take the roof,' said Johnny, hoisting himself up and clambering past Gunny. 'Where'd you find this?' he asked as slid on to the flat rooftop and gave a nod to Bear Claw.

'Hidden out back of the stables. I was up there getting the Black Maria ready when I spotted her under a mess of tarps. Seemed a better bet all around when I heard the shooting.'

'Is Joanna OK?'

'Sure. Last I saw of her she was on her way down to help out at the mine.'

'Right, then let's go.'

With a crack of his whip and a hefty slap of the reins bunched in his gauntleted hands, Gunny hollered and the stage heaved away. The six matching black stallions jumped forward with an obvious eagerness to go and brought the streamlined vehicle quickly up to a fair speed pace.

'How'd it go at the Coal Agency?' shouted Johnny to Bear Claw, above the noise of the pounding hoofs.

'Not so good for Len,' Bear Claw called back. 'Stopped one in the neck. Bled out whilst I held them off. I nailed two but the others got off with the gold.'

Johnny shook his head in sympathy,

he knew Len and Bear Claw had been good friends. 'We'll get some payback,' he said.

'You can bet your boots on that one,' agreed Bear Claw grimly.

Howling a loud 'Hah!' Gunny whipped the stage up to speed and the coach flew over the wide-open road out of Julesville. Johnny hung on to the luggage rails to keep himself in place as the stage slipped from side to side, wallowing hard on the bends as the steel reinforcing strained the double-strength leather suspension to its limits.

'We going to catch up with them?' shouted Johnny at Gunny's bent back.

'Not right off,' Gunny flew over his shoulder. 'But we'll catch 'em.'

Johnny recognized the determination in his voice and was sure then that Gunny was back with them again. He was in the place he knew best, at the back end of six streaming horses with the wind hard in his face and a trail of burning dust flowing out behind him.

Usually, Gunny would coax his team

on more gently, thinking of the long miles that lay ahead on a normal stage run but, their quarry having a short lead on them, he knew he could whip maximum effort from the horses to run down the outlaws. The team responded well, their sleek hides glowing glossily over their flexing muscles as they galloped and ate up the road.

Then, almost on cue, Gunny launched into a verse of his beloved 'Lorena'.

Dammit! Don't that beat all, thought Johnny. *Not now. Please, Gunny, not now.*

28

'I see them!' called Bear Claw.

There they were, just disappearing over a rise ahead. Seven scattered riders, small on the horizon.

'Must have thought they was clear,' growled Gunny. 'Not by a long chalk, my friends. Gunny Sack Debreau is hard on your tail.'

Johnny beat on the rooftop and hung over the edge to let Slade know. 'We see them!' he shouted down as Slade's upturned face appeared at the open window below.

'About time,' Slade called back. 'I feel like a damned Mexican bean in here. Jumping and popping all over the place.'

'Hang on,' said Johnny. 'Won't be long now.'

'Won't be too soon for me,' howled Slade, falling back inside as they hit another dip.

They left the road still in wild pursuit, the ground turning bumpy and uneven with twists and turns that it took all of Gully's skill to anticipate. Inevitably their speed slowed considerably and Johnny feared they would now lose the nimbler ponies of the raiders as they forged ahead.

This was where the stage was a disadvantage, but the vehicle had been constructed with such extreme difficulties anticipated and rode the rough ground well despite the discomfort of its occupants.

Evening was approaching now after a long hot day and the horizon was turning a soft shade of violet whilst shadows formed quickly in the gullies and draws as they rode through them. The dust behind them turned ochre-red in the setting sun and high above the great empty bowl of sky darkened. Everything around them in the rocky, dust-filled wilderness turned burnt gold in colour as the stage lurched and twisted over the uneven ground.

An hour of such travel passed and Johnny was about to give up and beg for a halt, his whip lash wounds aching so much from the continual sliding and battering he was receiving on the rooftop. Then they heard it.

'Gunfire!' called Bear Claw.

'What's that about?' asked Johnny.

'It's up ahead,' shouted Gunny. 'Must be them fellers.'

'Indians, do you think?' asked Bear Claw.

'That ain't wild shooting, that's rapid, regular firing. Sounds more like military,' said Gunny, hauling on the reins and slowing the team to walking pace.

'Hold up, Gunny,' called Slade from the window. 'Let's hear this.'

Obediently, Gunny drew the sweating horses to a fretting standstill and they all remained silent as they strained to make sense of the distant popping of rifle and small arms.

'Hell of a gun battle,' observed Bear Claw.

'You think them fellers had a falling out?' asked Gunny.

'I hear a long-range Sharps there. None of them boys carried a Sharps, they all had Winchesters,' supplied Slade as he stepped down from the coach.

'Well,' said Johnny. 'Somebody's laying into them. Let's head on and see it.'

'On foot,' ordered Slade. 'It's not far off; we can make it at the trot. Anyways, I'll be only too glad to get out of this bone-shaker before my limbs drop off.'

There was a general consensus on that score, except for Gunny who frowned at the implied criticism.

'Hell you say,' he muttered. 'She rode like ice on warm glass, you ask me.'

As the firing died out, they set off silently at the run in the gathering gloom, spread out in a forage line. Gunny had stayed to tie off the Titan team; then, leaving the snorting horses and noisy jingling of the loose harness behind he followed, shotgun in hand.

They ran through 1,000 yards of scrub and loose rock before reaching a high, regularly curved thirty-foot mound, its peak black against the dimming sky. The smooth sided mound was covered in deep, fine-grained sand and their boots sank into the soft material, making climbing difficult. Panting, they reached the rim and looked cautiously over.

Signs of the recent battle lay everywhere on the broad flat top of the rise. Bodies and fallen horses sprawled stiffly around the base of a lone flatbed wagon standing with a team of two. One of the team whickered, its head hanging low with the reins draping loose over the sprung driver's seat.

Beside the wagonette two men crouched over a small buffalo-chip fire; behind them a glinting Sharps carbine and a Winchester rifle were leaning against the wall of the flatbed. The men were delving into a pile of large saddle-bags set in front of them and were obviously well pleased with the contents.

Johnny recognized them instantly and hissed a long sigh of despair.

'What is it?' whispered Slade, who lay alongside him.

'It's my brothers,' spat Johnny bitterly. He sighed as he made his decision. 'You fellers stay here. I'll go talk to them.'

Before there could be any arguments with his decision, Johnny got to his feet and called out. 'Hey, boys! Adam. Billy Boy . . . it's me, Johnny. I'm coming in, so don't you shoot me.'

The two brothers turned quickly at the sudden noise, snatched up their weapons and pointed them towards the sound of the voice calling out of the darkness.

'Steady, boys. It's me, your brother Johnny. Hold on now.' Johnny walked forward, his hands held high.

'Hell, Johnny,' cried Billy Boy with a grin as he recognized Johnny. 'How in damnation did you get here?'

Adam rose to his feet, the Sharps still held in Johnny's direction. 'Brother

Johnny ain't alone, I reckon,' he observed quietly, his eyes quartering the darkness.

'Is that right, Johnny?' said Billy sadly. 'You come here with a posse?'

Johnny ignored the question as he closed upon them.

'What happened here?' he asked, waving a hand around at the fallen outlaws. One body caught his eye and he looked again at the crushed round-topped hat, cavalry trousers and moccasins. He thought he recognized the blood stained clothing from somewhere, but it slipped his mind as Billy Boy chuckled, his eyes alight with glee.

'They didn't want to part with their ill-gotten gains so we had to use a little leverage, ain't that right, Adam? You seen what's in these saddle-bags, Johnny? It's a pure fortune. I tell you, I've never seen so much gold.'

'You two took out all seven of them?' Johnny asked incredulously.

'The element of surprise,' said Adam dourly. 'Works wonders.'

'Where's your crew?' asked Johnny.

'Oh, they'll be to hand,' answered Adam vaguely. 'How about yours?'

'They'll be watching.'

'Johnny boy,' said Adam, shaking his head sadly.

'I told you to stay away,' snapped Johnny in reply.

'Apologize for that but this one was too good to miss.'

A moan issued from inside the wagon bed and a dark shape shuffled there.

'Who's that?' asked Johnny.

'That,' said Adam, 'would be their connection, ours and theirs. He had a little bump on the head during the fracas. Sounds like he's about to make a return to us now. I think you know the feller, Johnny.'

Johnny went round to the tail end of the wagon and looked in. Even in the shadowed interior he recognized the fat belly and fine white suit.

'Boss Lassiter,' he breathed.

'Seems you gave him a real pasting,' said Adam with a smile. 'He's no friend to you and that's for sure. Can't say I blame you though, fellow thinks an awful lot of himself. Was in my mind to dim his light the minute this business was over anyway.'

Lassiter pulled himself sluggishly to a sitting position, one hand clutching his head. 'Oh, my,' he murmured. 'What the hell happened?'

'Just a crease, fat man,' supplied Adam. 'Come on, wake yourself up. Look here, someone to see you.' Lassiter peered into the darkness, trying to focus on the figure before him.

'You!' he snarled. 'How'd you get here?'

'That's enough palaver, you boys!' the sharp order interrupted them, coming from the perimeter of the firelight. The three turned to see Slade, Gunny and Bear Claw standing in a tight semicircle and covering them. 'Shed the load,' said Slade, waving at their weapons.

With a sorry glance at Johnny, Adam slipped his pistol from its holster and tossed it and the Sharps to the ground.

'Do as he says, Billy Boy. They got us cold.'

Billy sucked his teeth, 'Oh, boy,' he said. 'I surely don't like doing that.'

'Do it!' snapped Slade. 'Johnny's brother or no, I'll drop you where you stand if you don't.'

'He means it,' said Johnny, resting his hand on Billy Boy's wrist. The boy dropped his weapons.

Johnny could hear Lassiter shuffling restlessly; he turned to see the man staring white-faced at Slade.

'Marshal,' Lassiter begged. 'It ain't what it seems. I'm only here in a protective capacity.'

'Sure,' drawled Adam cynically. 'Making sure all that cash gets into the right hands.'

'He's kidding, I know,' said Lassiter. 'But it's true. I'm representing Mr Martin here. Mr Martin of the Mercantile Bank. I'm here to see it all gets back to its rightful owners.'

'That a fact?' sniggered Billy Boy.

'Not what we heard.'

'It's true, I tell you,' shouted Lassiter. 'You ask him, he'll tell you.'

'We'll see about that back in town,' said Slade, turning his attention to Adam. 'Where's the rest of your gang, Cable?'

Adam wrinkled his nose and grinned. 'Oh, here and there,' he said.

'They're not anywhere,' Lassiter burst out spitefully. 'These two are here on their own. Couldn't bear to share the loot with the rest of them, could you?'

'That a fact?' said Slade. 'Well, makes it kind of awkward for you, Cable, doesn't it?'

Adam turned and fixed Lassiter with a stare that would have turned flesh to stone if it were able. 'You just signed your death warrant, fat boy,' he said coldly.

'Where do you stand on all this, Johnny?' Slade suddenly asked him directly.

Johnny bit his lip, subduing the feeling of betrayal that arose in him.

'I guess they go in for fair trial. I see

it go any other way, though, and maybe I'll think differently.'

Billy Boy crinkled his face. 'Aw, Johnny. Don't be like that,' he said.

'I'll see it goes right and proper, Billy Boy,' Johnny assured him.

'Maybe they'll hang us, though,' said Billy.

'Maybe,' agreed Johnny with a slight shrug.

'Fair enough, Johnny. It'll be done right, I'll see to that,' promised Slade. 'Now, let's get this gold loaded and pull on back to town.'

They put the two Cable brothers and Lassiter in the Titan. Bear Claw was detailed to drive the loaded flatbed and it was he who led the way back to Julesville. Slade felt duty bound to stay with the gold; he sat up riding shotgun alongside Bear Claw, but with his attention and rifle firmly fixed on the prisoners in the stagecoach behind. Johnny climbed up to his old position beside Gunny and they set off into the dark night.

'You did real well tonight, partner,' he said to Gunny as they started out.

'Some things you just don't forget,' Gunny grunted. 'Sorry it had to come to this though. Between you and your brothers.'

Johnny sighed. 'Me too. Guess they made their own beds and now they have to lie in them.'

'Don't despair. Maybe it'll turn out better than you think,' said Gunny. Johnny recognized the old man's attempt to cheer him up, just as he had on their stageline runs together.

'I sure hope so.'

Both vehicles drove at an easier pace on the way back, which gave Johnny time to thoughtfully consider his difficulties. He watched the passing dark shapes of the desert around them, green like an underwater landscape under the moonlight, but could still see no clear path ahead for himself and his brothers. He hated having to bring them in but mournfully recognized that his first duty lay with the office he had signed up for. Then, when they were still nine miles out from the town, they all saw the rusty red glow from Julesville lighting up the night sky.

'See that?' Slade called back. 'Mine's still burning.'

'Must be the coal set alight,' answered Gunny. 'That'll burn from now to kingdom come.'

Johnny nodded agreement. 'Might be the end of coalmining in Julesville for a while if they don't get it put out.'

Gunny nodded sourly. 'That won't go out, it'll get underground. Follow the seam and go on burning for years. I seen it once up in the Appalachians. No way to stop it.'

'What're you saying, Gunny? That we're looking at the end of Julesville?'

'Could be.'

'Say,' piped Johnny sarcastically, 'you got any more good news for me?'

'Sure,' Gunny wheezed. 'You've still got a murder charge and jail sentence hanging over you, partner, and there's no way to top that.'

29

Chaos was reigning when they arrived back at Julesville. The streets were still alive with people intent on helping the wounded from the colliery. Torches set on high poles burned around a temporary hospital that had been set up under canvas sheeting on the outskirts of the lower town.

There the wounded and dead were laid out in files beneath the canvas. The terrible display of the bodies of small children covered with blankets lying next to their adult fellow workers was a sad sight to Johnny as he stumbled down to the lower town in search of Joanna.

He found her amongst the moaning victims of the blast; her dress was covered in coal dust and she looked obviously exhausted. Joanna rushed into his arms at sight of him.

'Thank God,' she breathed. 'It's so

terrible Johnny. So terrible.'

He liked the feel of her as she ran into his embrace; despite the taint of dust and smoke coating her hair, she felt like she belonged there, cupped fittingly in the circle of his arms.

'Is this all of them?' asked Johnny, looking over her shoulder at the huddles of relatives and friends treating their own by the flickering light of the torches.

'Yes, twenty-three survived with broken bones and split heads. Nine are dead though.' Joanna sighed. 'There were so many young ones.'

'And the mine?'

'Still smouldering. They say they'll have to infill and cover the bench to shut off the burning coal. It's doubtful whether that stretch will ever be worked again though.'

'How're you holding up?'

They separated and she brushed a dirty hand over her forehead. 'Tired is all,' she said. 'But where have you been? They said there was shooting up in the town?'

'The mine was all a cruel diversion. A gang tried to take the banks.'

'Did they get away?'

'No, we caught up to them and retook the money; but there is bad news, I'm afraid.'

She waited curiously for him to answer.

'My brothers and Lassiter are involved, the marshal has them held in the jail-house.'

'Oh, Johnny, that is bad.'

'Well, we'll see how it pans out, but right now let's get you home and cleaned up. You look like you're all in.'

As they walked slowly up the dimly lit yet still busy streets to their lodgings at the edge of the upper town, Joanna took his arm and rested her head on his shoulder. It evoked a warm sense of belonging in Johnny and he decided not to spoil the moment by saying anything further of his own continuing problems.

'There is something I must tell you, Johnny,' she murmured.

'Uhuh, what's that?' he said, patting

her hand affectionately.

'We are to have a little one of our own.'

Johnny stopped suddenly. 'A baby! You are with child?'

She smiled shyly. 'The doctor confirmed it some days ago.'

'Why . . . why didn't you tell me before?'

'Because . . . ' she paused, 'well, you have so many other things on your mind. But now, with all this going on,' she waved a hand in the direction of the hospital behind them. 'All this awful despair and death, it seems a good time to tell you. For you to hear something hopeful, I mean.'

He enfolded her and kissed her lightly on the lips. 'I am blessed,' he whispered. 'No, *we* are blessed. It is the most wonderful of news.'

They stood that way for some time clasped in each other's arms in the middle of the street whilst torch-bearing townsfolk rushed unheeding around them like a fiery river around a rock.

30

'Bailiff, say your piece,' ordered the judge with a stern look at Bear Claw Charlie, who had been primed for the role earlier.

Bear Claw duly did his part by rote, stumbling over a few of the words: 'Come here and pay heed all ye who have business before the court, this here the District Court of Julesville in Polk County is called to order. Judge Asa Bowie Samples presiding.'

Judge Samples was an itinerant circuit judge who travelled a territory covering some 98,000 square miles over a year, dispensing justice amongst the scattered towns and homesteads. As such he was naturally eager to press on over his long route and was known to be swift with his sentencing, brooking little distraction from either verbose prosecutors or pleading defendants. An avuncular-looking but no-nonsense sort of man, he wore a black gown overcoat, a goatee beard and a favourite beaver-skin top hat on his head.

The court was being held in the town church, the only place big enough to hold all the interested population, who crowded its bench seats and stood in the aisles until the church was full to overflowing.

'Let's get on with it then,' the judge bawled from his podium, slamming down his gavel loudly. He had been placed before the simple altar, with a high-backed chair and the pastor's dining table brought in for the occasion. 'What've we got first off?'

Jack Slade rose to his feet. 'What we've got here, Judge, is an attempted bank robbery — '

'Hold on there!' interrupted the judge, slamming down his hammer again. 'Who the devil are you? State your full name and title.'

'Sorry, Judge,' apologized Slade. 'Marshal Jackson . . . ' he paused a moment in embarrassment, as if he had no real desire to expose his middle names, 'um . . . Everet Constadine Slade, town police officer.'

'Right, Marshal you have to identify yourself for the record, there's a regular form of procedure we have to fulfil here, y'see?' said the judge. 'Proceed.'

'These three men,' Slade indicated the row of prisoners, seated together on a bench alongside Johnny who was acting as their guard, 'were involved in an attempt to raid the three banks we have here in town.'

The judge nodded and sank back in his seat, his chin resting on his chest.

'During the course of which an explosion was set off at the coalmine as diversion, causing much death and destruction amongst the miners.'

'These here fellows did that?' asked the judge.

'Not directly, sir,' answered Slade. 'It was another gang that actually planned and carried out the raid. We downed some of the villains in town and I lost two deputies in the course of that gunplay. The rest of the gang made off and we gave chase but found them already dead, shot down in cold blood by those two Cable brothers sitting there.'

Judge Samples looked sourly at Adam and Billy Boy.

'Stand up, you two,' he ordered. Slowly the brothers stood up. Billy Boy's face was wreathed in smiles at this moment of public attention and he glanced around the courtroom cheerfully. Adam, more sombre, rose to meet the judge's stare with one of his own of equal seriousness.

'How'd you boys want to plead on that score?' asked the judge.

'Oh, we did it all right, Judge,' said Billy Boy brightly. 'Shot down everyone of them no accounts.'

'We was just helping out,' cut in Adam quickly. 'Seeing as they was bank robbers of ill fame we intended to do our civic duties and help out on the side of law and order.'

Billy Boy chuckled and nudged Adam in the ribs.

'That a fact, Marshal?' asked the judge, turning to Slade again.

'No, sir,' supplied Slade. 'They were just taking out the competition and intended to make off with the gold coin themselves.'

'And this other man here?' the judge said, waving his gavel at Lassiter.

'That there is Mr Lassiter, known as 'Lash' Lassiter, a saloon-keeper here in town. He was found at the scene and has some part in all this, but what that might be I haven't figured out yet. Says he was acting on behalf of one of the banks, the Martin Mercantile.'

The judge looked doubtfully at Lassiter. 'Well, what have you to say?'

Lassiter quickly rose to his feet. 'It's the truth, Judge. I have nothing to do with this other than acting on behalf of the Mercantile. Sent out by Mr Martin himself to track down and return his stolen monies. Sir, I'm an ex-employee of the Territory; why, I was a prison official at Gomar penitentiary — '

'Enough,' snapped the judge. 'You have any proof of what you say? Some directive from the bank, someone to go witness for you?'

'I'm sure Mr Martin will uphold my every word,' said Lassiter with an obsequious grin.

'He here?' asked the judge. Slade looked around the crowded courtroom until he spotted Martin, looking a little uncomfortable, seated amongst the front rows. Slade crooked a finger and Martin rose pompously to his feet.

'You the bank man?' asked the judge.

'I am, sir, Carter F. Martin, proprietor and sole owner of the Martin Mercantile Bank here in Julesville. At your service, your honour.'

'Well said.' Judge Samples nodded approvingly, scratching at his goatee. 'See, Marshal. Man identifies himself plain and simple, then everybody knows where they are. Now, Mr Martin, you've heard the claims of this fellow Lassiter. How say you; true or false? No need to elaborate, just a simple yes or no will do.'

Martin gave Lassiter a glancing look and tugged at his waistcoat, pulling it down over his ample stomach. 'Don't know the fellow; never saw him before this day.'

'What!' cried Lassiter angrily. 'Why d'you say that, you lying jackass? All you had to do was confirm me as your agent — '

Samples's gavel came down hard. 'Enough!' he roared. 'I'll abide no rough language in my court, d'you hear? You restrain yourself, sir, or I'll have you gagged.'

'But it's a lie, your honour,' pleaded Lassiter, sweat breaking out on his brow. 'Martin's the one set this whole thing off.'

A riffle of whispering broke out amongst the watchers at this, and Judge Samples smacked the table top again.

'Silence!' he bellowed and the room quietened. 'On your feet, Mr Martin,' he called to Martin, who had already sat down again. 'Now then. What's this? The man says you engineered the whole affair.'

'Can't think why he should say that, your honour,' Martin said calmly. 'Except as a means of justifying his situation. Why on earth should I rob my own bank?'

There was a hum of agreement throughout the court as the good sense struck home on that one.

'I suggest,' Martin went on, self-importantly, 'that this falsehood is merely a shallow fabrication made in a poor attempt to discredit myself and bring attention away from the real guilty party. Namely, Mr Lassiter himself. Who is doubtless the instigator of the whole sorry scheme.'

Lassiter was obviously furious, his skin colour changing to purple as he fumed at the accusation. With vengeful calm he faced Martin, his voice quivering as he spoke.

'Very well, Mr Martin. You won't cover me, then I'll tell it all. I'll not go down alone. It was me he set up,' Lassiter pointed a shaking finger at Martin. 'I was to go between him, his band of fellow bankers and the raiders. They all planned investment in a nefarious arms deal, the whole set of them. They was to use the banks' money to buy arms and sell them at a profit; least, that's what he told his partners. But old Martin there had other plans: a means of getting the whole bundle for himself. He planned it so the money transfer was to be held up by bandits, so he asked me to find him the men to do it.

'You see, Mr Martin there has a predilection for some of my cot girls. He might act like Mister High and Mighty but he's just like the rest of us really, so when he says he don't know me he's lying through his teeth. He knows me well enough — and Big Martha and Rawbone Kate, isn't that right, Mister Big Shot?'

Martin, who until now had been relying on what he considered to be a protected position, was surprised and disconcerted by the frank exposure of his more lascivious inclinations. He was colouring now, his face unmoving, and his body frozen.

'Be still, you fool,' he hissed. 'How can you say such things? Don't listen, I beg of you, your honour. I am an upstanding and respected member of this society; there is no way on God's good earth that I could ever be considered to be involved in such an underhand plot.'

'That a fact?' jeered Lassiter, getting into his flow now the lid was off. 'That why you asked me to find Joey Tuppence and get him to round up enough *hombres* to lift the load? Then go see the Cables here and get them to cut down that particular overhead once they'd done their part.' Lassiter turned to the assembled court. 'It was a way, you see? Of using all you folks' money supposedly for the arms deal, but instead of going through with the deal the real plan was to rob his own partners of their set-up fee, take it all for himself and blame the robbers for the whole deal.'

The roar that followed this was deafening; the church walls shook with the cries of anger and Judge Samples hammered the table top repeatedly in a vain attempt to achieve silence. It took a round fired ceilingward from the marshal's gun to regain some semblance of order.

'Thank you, Marshal,' said the judge, running his finger around his overheated collar. 'Drastic but warranted. Any more of that rowdiness and you'll all get out. This court will be cleared, you understand me?'

A ripple of muttering met this threat and the judge went on. 'Now then, we have here a confession of collusion, it appears. Marshal, take the man Martin into custody until this is settled. Put him on the bench next to the others. Damnedest mess I've ever heard.'

Slade quickly pulled the protesting Martin from the body of the court and deposited him unceremoniously next to the defendants, who moved along to make room for him. Johnny took the opportunity to look across at Joanna and Gunny in the front row. Their eyes met and Johnny raised his eyebrows in wonder at Lassiter's confession, Joanna hid her lips behind her hand as she smiled in response.

'Go on,' ordered the judge as the court settled and Slade moved to resume his station in the aisle.

'This here banker,' said Lassiter, jerking a thumb at Martin, 'was unlucky. He reckoned the raiders would take out the cash money once it was in the Titan stagecoach bound for the traffickers, all according to plan. He never reckoned on Joey Tuppence's part in it. Joey was a military man and to his way of thinking it would be far easier to hit the banks in town, where the cash was sitting pretty, over and above a running battle with a coach full of guards along a route he wouldn't be sure of until the day. So he took in mind to blow up the coalmine and distract folk whilst he hit the banks. He didn't reckon on Marshal Slade or his deputies being the problem they turned out, though,' Lassiter cast a sly sidelong glance at Johnny. 'Like our brave boy here, Deputy Johnny Dollar, so called. Although in reality I should tell you that this man is a lately escaped convict with a murder charge still laid against him.'

Once more a rustle of surprise ran around the court.

'Seeing as we're fanning the breeze here,' continued Lassiter with a sneer, 'let's hear it all, huh? That's right, folks. Your beloved deputy, Johnny Dollar, has a record of crime. He escaped from Gomar pen some years back, where he was serving a life sentence for murder. He killed two guards and three prisoners on his way out into the bargain. I should know, I was head guard there at Gomar during that time.'

A deathly silence came over the court

and, despite Lassiter's lying exaggeration, Johnny's gaze dropped to his boots and his shoulders slumped.

'See,' Lassiter whispered spitefully to Johnny. 'If I'm going down I'm about to take you all with me. Every last one of you.'

'You finished now, Mr Lassiter?' asked the judge.

'I've said my piece,' admitted Lassiter. He sat down.

'Deputy Dollar, do you have anything to say?'

Johnny rose slowly. He looked first at Joanna, his eyes full of sadness, then back at the judge.

'I — ' he began, but he was interrupted as the church doors flew open with a loud bang, sending those standing at the back flying in all directions.

A group of heavily armed men forced their way in. In the lead, waving an ugly cut-down scattergun, grinned the toothless features of Pete Medly.

'Nobody even breathe wrong!' he bellowed.

Slade rose quickly but, with a collective cocking of weapons, all the gang's dark muzzles swung towards him. 'Especially not you, Marshal,' warned Pete.

Slade froze where he stood.

Pete thrust his way down the aisle, pushing onlookers aside roughly. 'Come on, you Cables. We're about to get you out of here this instant.'

Billy Boy jumped to his feet. 'Wahoo!' he cried. 'You're a sight for sore eyes, Pete.'

'Just you hold on there!' shouted the judge angrily. 'You don't come into my courthouse waving pistols and giving orders. Who the hell do you think you are?'

The judge had seen a great deal in his time as circuit judge, and had experienced many extraordinary events in his courts of law, but even though he was well used to such displays he still felt, for his own pride's sake, that it was necessary to demonstrate some public objection to this offence against his office.

'Why, Judge,' said Billy Boy, laughing boldly. 'I'm Curly Bill Cable, this is my brother Adam, and these boys here are the Hellblazing Gang.'

'That's the truth, right enough,' agreed Adam, pushing his way along the length of the narrow bench and into the aisle alongside Pete. He looked down at Johnny, 'Come on, Johnny; there's nothing here for you now.'

'Yeah, come along,' agreed Billy Boy, patting Johnny on the shoulder as he passed him. 'Time to be one with us.' He looked around the courtroom and for once dropped his façade of foolishness. 'You folks are all damned fools, you know that? You don't know an honest man when you find one.'

Johnny looked up at them. 'Appreciate the offer but sorry, boys,' he said. 'I can't go with you.' He looked over at Joanna quickly to reassure her, then back at them. 'You sure you want to do this?' he asked.

'Hell!' Adam laughed. 'I really don't want to stay around here for no necktie party, brother. Well, if you ain't coming with us here's luck to you, because we're on our way now.'

With that he turned on his heel and, with Billy and Pete following, brushed his way through the onlookers and out to the church doors. Billy looked up at Slade and gave a cheeky wink as he passed.

'See you around, Marshal,' he promised.

'Don't nobody poke your heads out of this door for a while. Might get it blowed off,' Adam said. Then he slammed the double doors shut.

As the doors closed, bedlam started up amongst the crowd in the chapel. Slade pushed his way quickly to the front.

'Come on, Bear Claw. You too, Johnny, we'll use the side door.'

'What are you about, Marshal?' asked

the judge, raising his voice over the row.

'No time, Judge. We've got to get them in the street.' With that Slade ran out through the altar side door with Bear Claw behind him. Johnny had just risen to follow them when he heard a cry behind him.

'Johnny!' Gunny called desperately. Johnny turned to see Lassiter holding Joanna before him. The crowd fell back as he pointed a small two-shot derringer to her head. Lassiter peered at Johnny over Joanna's shoulder as he backed away down the aisle.

'Don't even think on it, Dollar,' he shouted. 'Anybody try and stop me and I'll put one through her brain.'

Johnny tensed. 'Where'd you get that pistol?' he asked.

'I fear it is mine,' said the banker Martin sheepishly from where he still sat at the defendants' bench. 'I carry one always. The lying scum said we could both get out with it.'

'Oh no, you're staying right here, Martin,' growled Lassiter. He backed up the aisle, still holding Joanna in a tight grip, one arm locked around her throat. 'I'm not doing you any favours after you turned on me. You can take all the heat coming down for this on your lonesome.'

Johnny and Gunny followed as Lassiter pushed the doors open behind him and went out into the street. A crowd followed after them, pushing and shoving to see what was happening but the sound of loud gunshots quickly drove them back inside.

Gunfire was echoing down the street from nearby. As Johnny reached the lower town crossroads he saw Slade and Bear Claw standing in the centre of Main Street, their arms raised and both men firing their pistols steadily after the departing outlaws, who were leaving a cloud of dust behind them as they rode fast out of town.

'Slade! Bear Claw!' called Johnny as Lassiter backed away hurriedly, dragging Joanna past them down the street towards the lower town. But the two lawmen were too busy looking the other way; Johnny's call to them was lost in the sounds of their shooting.

'It's up to us,' said Gunny at his elbow.

Johnny stared at him with fixed, glazed eyes, a mixture of fear and concern showing. 'If he does anything to her, I'll . . . I'll . . . ' He said no more as he took off quickly after the two as they vanished between the buildings around the lower town.

'Tell Slade,' he called to Gunny over his shoulder as he hurried off.

The streets were deserted, most folks attending the trial or still working steadily at covering the smouldering mine. As Johnny ran after the two disappearing figures, the sounds of the shooting followed him. It was an eerie sound amongst the vacant façades of the buildings and the hollow empty alleyways. Grimly, as he approached the Eureka Loophole, Johnny checked the load on his pistol, spinning the chamber and looking down at the shine of brass.

Johnny carried a Colt with a longer barrel than a normal gun-fighter, it was the seven-and-a-half-inch so-called 'Cavalry' barrel length. Not so swift on the draw but with a forty-gram black powder load, he knew he could send sixteen and a half grams of blunt-nosed lead with deadly accuracy. A bullet that could wreak terrible effects on the human body.

Johnny carried it now, drawn and down by his side as he stepped up on to the sidewalk, his footsteps sounding hollow on the boards. Inside, he heard the sounds of panicked scrabbling. As he slowly pushed open the batwing doors he saw Lassiter shoving handfuls of paper money into an open carpetbag.

Joanna stood leaning back fearfully against the bartop, a thickset, rock-steady barman covering her with a shotgun from behind the bar. Joanna's eyes were wide with fear as she watched Lassiter.

Johnny stepped into the bar room

and let the doors swing back noisily behind him.

'Stand away, Joanna,' he said.

'Oh, Johnny,' she gasped as she saw him. Lassiter whirled, his own Colt now in his hand.

'Keep her covered,' Lassiter snapped to the barman and the man dutifully swivelled the shotgun. 'Best lay it down, Dollar,' said Lassiter. 'I'll have her blown apart, I swear I will.'

'Just you and me,' said Johnny coldly.

'No, no, oh no.' Lassiter shook his head. 'That's not the way of it. Your lady's going to be my free ride out of here. Now, lay that shooting iron down.'

'You,' said Johnny to the bartender. 'Put up that double barrel if you want to live. I won't give you a second chance.' His voice was hard and level without a hint of doubt and the barman hesitated at the sound of such dangerous confidence. The barrel wavered and lowered a fraction as the barman was lost in indecision.

Then the shooting started.

Gunny stepped suddenly through the curtain at the back of the bar, shotgun in hand. He had come in through the back door, knowing full well the layout of the place.

Gunny put a blast in way of the bartender, who spun round, loosing off his own scattergun at the same time. The pellets ripped a jagged hole in the curtain next to Gunny, sending it billowing wildly like the sail of a ship in a high wind.

At the same moment, Lassiter fired at Johnny who stood alone in the centre of the room twenty feet away. Johnny coolly raised his Colt out before him, holding it straight and at arm's length. Bullets from Lassiter's pistol were winging around him, he could hear their crack as they passed close by his head. One plucked at his shirtsleeve but Johnny did not deviate as he slowly advanced towards Lassiter, firing steadily as he came.

Behind the bar, Gunny fired again with the other barrel of his shotgun. His load caught the barman in mid-turn, sending the man in a bloody tumble down the length of the bar. The man landed amongst a shatter of glassware as he upset the lower stock cabinet, pulling the bottle-stacked shelves down around him.

A bullet hit Lassiter in the shoulder. He screamed once in shock but in desperation lifted his gun arm and wildly fired again. Johnny continued on his merciless mission; two more of his bullets hit his opponent as he came on. Lassiter bucked back against the bartop roaring with pain and rage. One arm flailed out and caught the carpetbag, spilling dollar bills in a shower amongst the powder smoke.

Lassiter fell, his body bouncing hard against the bar as he went down. Johnny continued firing until his Colt was empty, the hammer clicking on dead brass. He felt only heat and the sting of cordite against his skin, his features hardening to rock as he stood over Lassiter. When he was sure

Lassiter was finished, he turned to look across at Joanna.

She stood frozen, one hand covering her mouth, and her terrified eyes open wide, staring at Johnny. Then she ran to him and he enclosed her tightly in his arms. The fear and tension fell away from him as he smelt her hair and felt the softness of her body hugging him.

Gunny rose from behind the bar, a full whiskey bottle in his hand.

'How about a celebratory noggin?' he asked with a crooked grin.

Johnny glowered at him over Joanna's shoulder. With a slow shrug, Gunny smiled and pushed the bottle away.

. . . and that's the true story of the life and times of Johnny Dollar, but not quite that of John Cable.

As it turned out, only one of the Hellblazers had been downed during the shoot-out following their escape. It was young Billy Cable who was shot through the back by Marshal Slade and

Bear Claw Charlie. His body was exhibited in front of the mortician's parlour for the populace to see and be photographed with. The photographer, who would sell anyone a print of the occasion for a few cents, was new to Julesville and had no way of knowing just who the felled outlaw really was. He did good business that day and was more interested in making money than the character of his subject.

When Marshal Slade told him he had been the middle of the three Cable brothers, the one also known as Johnny Dollar, he was none the wiser and dutifully scratched the name on the glass negative. The early photographic processes were primarily sensitive to blue light and Billy Boy's blond hair turned a darker shade, and took on the appearance of black curling hair instead of its natural colour in the prints.

So, what exists today in the archives is only a stained sepia-toned picture. The contrast is too bright and the edges are blurred, of a corpse propped in a tilted wooden box with a piece of card laid across the chest with the name crudely scrawled on it. This is believed to be the only recorded image that remains of Johnny Dollar, outlaw and killer.

Carter F. Martin, the banker, was run out of town later that same week, carried naked on a cross-tied beam, tarred and feathered by an angry mob with none of the town's police force taking a hand or doing a thing to stop it. Martin's fellow conspirators at the other banks lost their positions but, as is the way of all things concerning the banking community, they still worked for many years in finance, only in less obvious positions.

Adam Cable was brought down two weeks after the affair at Julesville, shot and mortally wounded in the street during an unsuccessful attempt on a Laramie bank. The Hellblazing Gang thereafter disappeared into history.

Of what followed for Johnny and Joanna Cable and Gunny Sack Debreau, there is only hearsay. Some say they travelled west over the Rockies to California, where they got into the hardware business, others that they eventually went north to the goldfields of Alaska to seek a fortune and that all trace of them vanished in the snow up there. One lady historian tracked down a certain Mr J. Cable to Panama City and to a mining conglomerate down there, but this is only a very loose connection which does not stand up to close scrutiny.

But there are Cables still living in Wisconsin. A tight family group in Dewar, Polk County claim descent from the surviving Cable brother. Oral family tradition says that Johnny and Joanna stayed where they were, had first a daughter and then a son and lived out their lives secretly in the Wisconsin Territory. Of Gunny, all that is known by them is an old bill of sale that the family keep treasured, in which it is stated that the Slade Haulage Line was bought up for a nominal fee of a dollar fifty, its new owner changing the *name and calling it Debreau's Haulage and Shipping.*

All that exists of Julesville today, is a ghost town. A few brick walls, crumbling ruins. The upper town slid down long ago during the winter storms into the lower town, the two parts mingling indistinguishably. The coalmining industry, ruined by the fire, left the town without income and over the intervening years the town, as do all things in this life, slowly faded into memory, eventually becoming no more than part of the landscape that surrounds it.

Other titles in the
Linford Western Library:

A NECKTIE FOR GIFFORD

Ethan Flagg

The bounty hunter known as 'Montero' learns that his brother is to be hanged for murder in the New Mexico town of Alamagordo. A single clue left by the dead man — the two letters 'MA' — ensures that a guilty verdict is inevitable. The two brothers had parted some years before under hostile circumstances, but Montero is convinced that Mace Gifford would never shoot a man in the back. He plans an ingenious escape, but saving his bother's neck is only the beginning — he has to find the real killer . . .

THE PHANTOM RIDER

Walt Keene

A mysterious killer is riding into each town on the plains, hell-bent on dispatching as many men, women and children as he can. In the blood of his victims is scrawled the same message: 'The Phantom'. As the ruthless horseman travels further south, he is unaware that he is soon to face three men who could be the ones to stop his unholy carnage. For Tom Dix, Dan Shaw and the legendary Wild Bill Hickok are waiting . . .

HIGH NOON IN SNAKE RIDGE

Scott Connor

Matthew Jennings returns to Snake Ridge to reconcile with his respectable family — and finds his brother lying dead. To track down the killer, he secures a position as deputy town marshal; but when he follows the evidence, it leads to a man who must be innocent: his own father. Even worse, a feuding outlaw gives him an ultimatum to leave town by noon, or die . . . Matthew's resolve to turn his back on his past will be tested to breaking point before he faces a high noon showdown.

TEAL'S GOLD

Abe Dancer

In the bed of a remote New Mexico creek, Austen Teal strikes gold. When the old placer miner is shot dead in a Calido Run gunfight, however, he has only managed to disclose a few cryptic words about its exact location to his young son. Five years on, Wesley Teal sets out to solve the riddle, in a quest to track down the source of his pa's gold. But he is being watched and trailed by hard cases who will stop at nothing to get the gold first . . .